Condemned to You

Marianna Buffolino

Iannotta
CREATIONS CORP

Contents

Chapter One   1

Chapter Two   4

Chapter Three   7

Chapter Four   11

Chapter Five   15

Chapter Six   22

Chapter Seven   34

Chapter Eight   38

Chapter Nine   43

Chapter Ten   51

Chapter Eleven   58

Chapter Twelve   63

Chapter Thirteen   72

Chapter Fourteen   76

Chapter Fifteen   82

Chapter Sixteen   86

Chapter Seventeen 94

Chapter Eighteen 100

Chapter Nineteen 104

Chapter Twenty 107

Chapter Twenty-One 109

Chapter Twenty-Two 114

Chapter Twenty-Three 121

Chapter Twenty-Four 126

Chapter Twenty-Five 130

Chapter Twenty-Six 132

Chapter Twenty-Seven 141

Chapter Twenty-Eight 150

Chapter Twenty-Nine 156

Chapter Thirty 161

Chapter Thirty-One 166

Chapter Thirty-Two 170

Chapter Thirty-Three 174

Chapter Thirty-Four 180

Epilogue 183

Author's Note 189

Chapter One

"What the fuck is going on!" The tone in Luca's voice was one that I'd never heard before.

Bethany snapped out of shock and sprang onto her knees, bowing in forgiveness as she pled, "Luca, please. Have mercy."

Getting to my feet, I watch Luca sneer at his sister then look to me. The look of betrayal in his eyes lasted a mere few seconds before it turned into pure rage. Lunging toward me, instant regret of my choice to continue seeing Bethany clawed within me. Although I was certain Luca would kill me right then and there, fighting for my life at the moment didn't seem worth it. I did this to myself and if death was the punishment, then so be it.

Luca's fist hit me straight in the jaw causing me to hit the ground. My face hit the wooden floor and the sound of a gun click sent a shiver down my spine.

"Luca! No!" Bethany screeched.

Luca ignored her. "Look at me!" He demanded from me.

Turning onto my back, I look up to meet my fate. Out of all the crazy shit I've done, never did I think I'd go out like this in a cowardly manner. I've made too good of a name for myself to have my life end like this. The torment in Luca's eyes made me ashamed. I was the one person he could trust wholeheartedly, the one person he never had to question.

Bethany was sobbing. "Please. Luca don't do it."

Rushing in were their mother and sisters who were shocked, speechless, and mortified at what they were looking at. Bethany naked sobbing on the sofa, while I lay naked on the floor with Luca pointing his gun at me. They didn't need to be told what had happened. Rita quickly threw a blanket over Bethany.

"Luca," their mother voiced, unsure whether she could tame the situation. "Not here."

Alfie enters the room, "How did Emilio get here so fast?" When he realized what was going on he stopped in his tracks.

"Alfie," Luca stated as he lowered the gun, "Take him to the box."

There was a sigh in the room from all the women except Bethany who threw herself onto me.

"NO!," She cried. "You can't!"

Yanking her by the arm, Luca pulled her off of me. "I should make you watch."

Pulling her arm out of his grip, she shouts, "I hate you Luca! Kill him and I'll kill myself!"

"I have a spare in the car," Luca replies holding his gun up.

"Luca!" The women shouted in unison.

The look of emotional damage in Bethany's eyes killed me. She stood there in shock. Her relationship with her brother had become quite strong the last few years, and Luca has lightened the reigns. Once she was married to Pio, Luca felt that the obligation of taking care of her fell onto her husband. This moment had forever destroyed their sibling bond. Bethany's sisters escorted her out of the room.

His mother, Nicoletta, stood looking at him with a loss for words. She didn't even bother looking at me. She was a kind woman to those she loved, which really were only her children and grandchildren – in her eyes the rest of us were just privileged to be around the DeCarlo family.

"Luca," she said calmly, "If Bethany takes her own life because of your actions, I will hold that against you til I die." She walked out of the room before Luca could respond.

"Alfie!" Luca shouted as he snapped his fingers.

Alfie looked like he jumped out of his skin and realized he was given a command he hadn't fulfilled. He rushed toward me helping me to my feet.

Placing his gun inside his holster under his suit jacket, Luca looked at me as though he didn't know me. I didn't say a word. What could I possibly say to make this less tense?

"E tu... Emilio." Shaking his head in disappointment, Luca waited for me to answer and when I didn't, he got angry. "Well! What do you have to say for yourself?!"

Sorry wasn't going to cut it. Neither was begging for forgiveness. For Luca, actions spoke louder than words and no words could repair the damage that had been done.

Chapter Two

I sat in the backseat of Alfie's Escalade, the cold leather seat against my skin sent chills through me. It was silent but each time Alfie looked in the rearview mirror at me, his eyes were full of questions. Questions to some things I didn't even have the answers to.

"You should have put me in the trunk," I voiced breaking the silence as I made eye contact with him through the mirror.

Mistake number one.

His eyes dart back and forth between the road and the rearview mirror. "Right," he sighed, "I just... didn't think I'd be in the position."

"What? Bringing me to my death sentence or driving a naked man in your car?"

"What do you want me to say E?" Alfie shook his head, "What were ya thinkin'?"

Looking out the window, I replied, "I wasn't thinking."

I ran my hand through my hair. My hands weren't even tied up.

Mistake number two.

I've always been tough on the kid and part of me likes to think he looked up to me, so to hear the shock of the situation in his tone told me I failed as a mentor. Since knowing he was a DeCarlo, I made it a point to focus on making him my protégé. Not to take my place but to be the best so no one would question why someone like him worked so closely with Luca. The secret he was really Marco's son never came to light and I never spoke a word that I knew the truth. The more I looked at Alfie the more he looked like his father who was someone I respected.

I took in the last moments I'd ever see my city. The sunlight fought through the blacked out windows as I ached for the light to hit my skin. It was a cold March day, but the sun was beaming in the sky. I could have lowered the window to feel the wind hit my face for the last time but the feeling in the pit of my stomach began weighing me down and I found myself holding back tears.

I clear my throat, "Cassie…" I couldn't even finish. The thought of my sister having to plan my funeral gutted me.

Alfie looked up to the rearview mirror, "I'll make sure she's okay."

"Make sure she leaves Chicago." This city was tainted enough for her, I didn't want her here for another second.

Alfie nodded his head. The realization of my absence weighed heavy on him and finally he let it show "Look E. I don't wanna to do this."

He was about to go on a rant so I cut him off, "You have to."

"How the hell am I gonna take your place?"

"If you follow what I've taught you, then you'll be fine."

"You and I both know I can't fill ya shoes."

"I know you love this family. So make sure you honor that. If you do can that, then you're on the right path."

Silence. The thought of Bethany and what she said made me want to vomit. There was no doubt in my mind that she would follow through on her words. If I left this earth, she'd soon follow after. I could jump out of this car right now, get both Bethany and Cassie then get the hell out of here. Alfie didn't even check to see if I was buckled in.

Mistake number three.

Just as I slowly put my hand on the lock, the sound of an engine roared so loud. Turning my head to look out the window, there was a back Escalade speeding right toward us. Before I could shout out to Alfie, the impact of the Escalade hitting us had me flying from one end of the backseat to the other. The sound of the impact rang through my ears, and I saw Alfie passed out in the driver's seat with blood dripping down his face. Quickly I grabbed the gun out of the console and cocked it back. This was a hit. Who the fuck would have the balls to do that in these streets?

The Escalade backed up and I saw someone get out. Quickly I lay low so that when the door opened, I could then pop up and get in a shot. The back door opened and I was ready to blow off the person's head, but when I pulled the trigger nothing happened. The gun wasn't loaded. Fuckin' Alfie. I kicked the person in the chest and lunged forward to jump out the Escalade only to meet a fist to the face.

Everything went black.

Chapter Three

The sound of Bethany panting and moaning became louder and louder as I alternated between massaging her clit with my tongue and sucking on it with my mouth. Her legs clamped together between my head as though that would stop me or delay her orgasm. The bed was soaked with her juices.

"Emilio, please," Bethany begged. "Fuck me."

I bit down on her clit causing her to squeal. "You didn't have enough last night?"

"Still not sore enough," Bethany bit her lip.

Her hands were bound together and tied to the headboard the entire night as she let me take her multiple times. I loaded her mouth and pussy with so much of my cum I was surprised it wasn't seeping out of her pores.

I put my head back down between her legs to finish her off. Just as always, she waited for my command.

"Ready to cum for me baby?"

She nodded her head, her eyes sparkling with excitement.

"Tell me," I demanded.

The words were barely out of her mouth before a stream of warm liquid flew out of her pussy and onto my face. I was completely covered in her juices. Pulling my head away, I watch it all flood down to her asshole. Slowly I press a finger to slide inside. Bethany lightly jolted in shock. It was tight and I was trying to loosen it up before I inserted my cock which was a lot bigger than my finger. With my thumb, I rubbed her clit to continue stimulation. As her body began to warm up again, I positioned myself on my knees. Bethany braced herself by holding onto the rails of the headboard.

Gripping my cock, I slowly entered her tight asshole until I was fully inside. Bethany's juices made it easier to push in although there was a hitch in her breathing as her body tightened and legs twitched. The discomfort written on her face as I had my way with her created this sense of mental stimulation that heightened my arousal. Dominance in the bedroom had always been a major factor in getting me off. Anal wasn't anywhere as pleasurable as vaginal sex, but for me the large part of the pleasure came from the dominance it gave me for Bethany allowing me to fuck her this way. The fact that it hurt her a bit and was something a good girl wasn't supposed to do; I liked that she let me do it anyway just to please me. Her submission to me for my pleasure made this feel better than it had any right to feel.

"You can go harder," Bethany breathed.

Her legs wrapped around my waist while her hands still held onto the headboard above her. Normally, I'd have a hand around her neck and another on her breast but I just wanted to take her all in. Both my hands held her hips as I watched her perfect breasts flop around. I'd never admit it out loud but I missed her and there wasn't going to be anyone or anything that would come between us. She was the only thing left in my life worth fighting for. My life was tossed upside down and inside out but Bethany was the only thing that wasn't taken away from me. after a few more pumps I finished and then hovered over her. She looked at me with those emerald eyes making me feel like a new man – erasing all the darkness within me. Those emerald eyes as green as moss. The way she looked at me as though I was the only thing that mattered.

The day was spent claiming her body over and over until the sun began beaming through the shades as it was beginning to set. I could spend the rest of my life without sleeping doing this over and over.

"I love you," she said placing a kiss on my lips.

As she pulled away, I placed my hand on the back of her head to pull her back in. "I love you more," I say against her soft pink lips. As she sat up, a ray of light hit her face making the dimple caused by her smile more noticeable. I found myself falling in love all over again. I pulled her onto me so that her head rested on chest as we lay there letting our bodies sync together. Her heart beat in perfect time with mine. Her hand found mine and our fingers intertwined, speaking words unspoken. Synced to one another, my heart exploded. I'd never be the same man again and I didn't want to be if it meant having a life with her. Without disrupting our position, I reached out to the nightstand, and pulled out a box from the top draw.

"Marry me," I said in a low calm voice as I opened the box to show the diamond ring.

Bethany lifted her head to look at me in surprise. "What?"

"Marry me," I repeated. "Bethany DeCarlo, I want you to marry me."

Her eyes sparkled and a wide smile crossed her face as she collided her mouth with mine.

"It's beautiful," she said as I put the princess cut 3 carat platinum ring on her finger.

"Is that a yes?" I smirked.

"Yes."

Suddenly my face felt wet and my eyes shot open as I sharply gasped for air to enter my lungs as I jolt awake. I froze at the click of a pulled back hammer to a gun that was pressed against the side of my head. The heat of the barrel against my head told me the gun was fired not too long ago, and I wasn't looking to be the next victim so I remained still as I sat in the seat of a dimly lit vehicle. All the windows were blacked out to the fullest. There were three men in here aside from myself. The man next to me holding the gun to my head, the driver, and someone in the passenger seat.

Chapter Four

"Well well," the male voice from the passenger seat traveled to the back seat, "Looks like the untouchable Emilio Pugliese isn't so untouchable after all." There was a slight Italian accent in his mature voice.

"Who the fuck are you?" I spat out.

"You'll learn soon enough. Until now. I need you gone."

"You can go fuck ya self."

The impact of the handle on the gun almost knocked me out again. Fighting through the pain and the darkness itching to consume my vision, I was ready to throw fists. What did I have to lose at this point? But before I had the energy to make a move, the man in the passenger seat spoke.

"Now is that a way to talk to someone who just saved your life?"

There was a calmness in his voice. It was clear he didn't fear me or the circumstance. Word of my downfall wouldn't have gotten out yet. Who was this man? What did he want from me?

"I didn't ask you to save my life," I replied irritated.

"I can have Birdy there right beside you make you sink to the bottom of Chicago's river."

"I know how this works. I'm dead either way."

"You need to be more optimistic Emilio."

"I'll add it to my new year's resolution."

"I've been keeping an eye on your Emilio. You have a set of balls on you."

"Yeah well, even with my shriveled-up dick in between my legs, there's no doubt I have the biggest pair in the car."

All three men laughed. I was still butt naked and the cold leather against my skin was uncomfortable. Being watched didn't concern me as much as the fact that no one, not even myself, picked up on it.

"What the hell do you want?" I asked.

"I think you'd make a great addition to the team."

"Team?" I had to hold back from a laugh. "What are you going to have me do trust falls with Birdy over here?"

"If you're interested, which you will be, then you'll take my offer."

"What makes you so sure I'll be interested in your offer?"

"If I don't kill you, surely, Luca will. At least under me, you'd have my protection."

"I rather retire."

"The protection would extend to your sister, Cassie. It'd be a shame if you had to bury another sibling."

The reference to my deceased sister Marie got under my skin. I couldn't care less what happened to me, but Cassie didn't deserve any more agony in her life.

"Leave Cassie outta this," I said, speaking through my teeth.

"I can, if you agree to work for me."

If you asked anyone, they would tell you I had no weaknesses. Whoever these men were seemed to know more than anyone should. That I'd risk my own life to save my sister wouldn't be surprising but to know where I was at that exact time and how defenseless I would be in that very moment wasn't some lucky guess. I was being watched. For how long, who knew but if I didn't even realize they were keeping tabs on me then without doubt they had the upper hand. That hasn't happened to me in years. I didn't know who they were or what they were capable of. My heart was beating so hard

I thought it was going to rip right out of my chest. I had no other choice but to give in.

"Doesn't look like I have much of a choice."

The man laughs, "There's always a choice. You just have to pick the right one."

I saw Birdy take his free hand and reach down in front of him. Pulling up a duffle bag, he tossed it to me and let it fall onto my lap.

"I'll reach out when it's time," the man said.

"And in the meantime?" I questioned.

"Get out of town."

We were at the entrance of the airport. Inside a duffle bag were black sweatpants with a hoodie, sneakers, a burner phone, a passport, and a wad of cash. After throwing on the clothes, I opened the passport to find a picture of my face with a different name.

"Jim Albertsson?" I mocked.

"Could have been Dicky Smalls," Birdy said as he pushed the barrel of the gun further into my head. His voice was raspy.

"Clever," I commented as I quickly got dressed.

We pulled up to the flight departures drop off.

"This is your cue to get out," Birdy stated.

No one outside would be able to see what was happening in the backseat. This was just another vehicle dropping off a person at the airport. When I opened my door, I quickly looked back in to see if I could see any one of their faces but the blaring sun in my face made it difficult.

I quickly ran into the airport. My heart was somehow pounding even harder at the thought someone would see me – that I would get caught before I even had a chance to leave.

Staring at the departure board to find which flight that would whisk me away from the life I'd known for the last 45years had me feeling lost.

Looking down at the passport, I opened it up and read the name again as though this wasn't really happening to me right now. No longer was I Emilio Pugliese. Anything and everything I'd think of would need to be erased so that I could take on this new identity – at least until I figured something out.

Walking up to the ticket desk, I smiled at the woman who greeted me. "Book me the next flight out of here."

She seemed confused. "Just anywhere?"

"I'm in an adventurous mood."

"Okay," she replied seeming excited.

There was nothing exciting about what was happening. She mumbled off some things but I couldn't get myself to even pay attention. All I could think about was Bethany. If she thought I was dead. How I was praying that she wouldn't take her own life just for me. Deep down I knew Bethany would follow through on that threat, and the feeling of grief hit me as though it was happening in real time.

"Mr. Albertsson[CJ6] , your total is $1,900."

I looked to the woman and placed down enough hundred dollar bills. As she handed me my boarding pass, I thanked her. I took a deep breathe.

New name. New location. New life. Here I go.

Chapter Five

The sound of the sensual music hummed in my ears as my eyes watched Athena crawling naked toward me. Her dark brown hair twisted in a braid, dragging on the floor around her hands. I'd done everything I could the last three months to get Bethany off my mind, but it was nearly impossible. My tastes in the bedroom had grown darker in spite of it. As she made her way to me, the grip of the chain I held in my hand tightened as I itched to wrap it around her neck. The feel of her hair around my toes sent a tingle of excitement through me. I stood above her looking down as she waited for her command. She knew not to speak unless she was spoken to or move unless I commanded it to be so.

"Kneel," I commanded as I walked behind her.

My erection sprang up toward her round face. Watching her eyes light up in excitement did nothing to me. Athena was the opposite of Bethany which was deliberate. Dark hair, curvy hips, and dark eyes – whatever it took for me to forget my Barbie bombshell. However, despite my attempts of putting my dick into various women, the only way I could finish was the memory of Bethany. It didn't even need to be sexual. The thought of her hair blowing in the wind, or the heartwarming look she would give me, or even picturing her long legs would send me over the edge. I missed her.

I curled the chains around her neck and squeezed a bit until her breath was shallower than the orgasm that escaped her mouth just moments ago.

Athena had been my escape the last three months, and she had allowed me to use her body any way I pleased.

Bending down, I got close to her ear as I lightly tugged on the chain and whispered in her ear, "You want more you filthy whore?" Lowering my mouth further down and biting down on her cheek, watching her body react so tenderly.

She tilted her head back so that we locked eyes. Her throat muscles slightly moved as she swallowed and her stare held a deep hunger to be ravished.

A smirk crossed her face. "Make this a birthday I won't forget."

My heart tightened and just like that my dick went limp. Fuck. That wasn't what I needed to hear today.

"It's your fuckin' birthday?" I spat out.

Athena nodded, "It is."

Letting go of the chains, I stepped back and looked for my pants. "Get the fuck out."

Stunned she looked at me, "Www... why? Have I upset you?"

Suddenly her Icelandic accent irritated me. "You should be spending your birthday with your husband." I pulled out a packet of cigarettes and lit one up.

"He's working. Why can't you make my birthday wish come true?" She got to her feet and walked toward me.

I put my hand out motioning for her to stop getting closer. "No," I said as I puffed out smoke from my mouth. "Out of all the days in the year, you had to be born today."

"Why are you being so cruel?" She replied, stunned by my comment.

Making my way out to my little balcony, the cold air hit my skin. When I landed here, I thought the cold would bother me. But the windy city of Chicago made the cold weather here in Iceland feel like a chilly breeze.

Maybe because my blood was boiled most of the time so my body was letting out heat and I barely felt the cold nipping at me. After finishing my smoke, I went back inside and poured myself a drink. Thankfully Athena left without much fuss.

Grabbing my phone off the counter, I made my weekly call. The conversation started as usual.

"Bless me Father for I have sinned."

"There's no sin too great for the Lord to forgive my child," the familiar voice responded.

"The Lord is good."

"All the time."

I heaved a sigh of relief. It was our secret code that I used to enquire if my sister was alright. Father Joel was an old friend of mine growing up. He chose a morally just path compared to mine. As a priest, he held his vow of secrecy. From Father Joel's response I felt a calmness knowing that Cassie was okay.

"I have prayed like you asked me to Father, yet nothing. Did the Lord speak to you about me?"

"He wants you to cast your burdens on Him because He cares for you always. No matter what it is that troubles you, you will find comfort under his wings. That's what the Bible said."

Another good news. Cassie was laying low due to the recent happenings. That was what he meant by "finding comfort under his wings." It was the best thing to do at least until the dust settled. He was also letting me know that there might be a breach in communication and I might not get any messages from my sister for a while since she was transferring to another hiding spot.

"I'm having trouble praying Father. My faith is testing me."

"Even though the devil is prowling around looking for whom to devour, you must hold fast to your faith. God always gives his children a second chance. After Nathan condemned David for stealing the most cherished lamb of a poor man, God still offered him a shot at redemption."

The code for Bethany was "Lamb" and he was telling me that she was attempting to overcome personal struggles. There was only so much Father Joel was able to get on Bethany. The only reason he had intel on Bethany was from Nicoletta, her mother, who spoke to Father Joel on a weekly basis – almost using him like a therapist. I'd been able to keep tabs on the family so well because I knew every place they went and everyone they interacted with.

"I'll pray harder Father."

"The Lord blesses you."

Tossing the phone back on the counter, I grabbed the drink I had poured for myself. Raising up a glass as though I had company, I cheered and saluted, "Happy Birthday Bethany."

The feel of Brennivín coats my mouth and I swallow it without a flinch. I wasn't a fan of the liquor here but I wasn't looking to be picky tonight. Opting to lose the cup, I grabbed the bottle of clear spirit and walked back outside. This time I grabbed a jacket. Sitting on the chair taking swigs of what the Icelandic natives here called the Black Death, I stared up at the sky. A mix of cigarette smoke and my breath swirled in the air around me as I adored the Northern Lights, casting a green light across the dark night sky. If my apartment wasn't located in a more isolated area, I might not be able to see them with the cast of city lights, but out here where it was dark, you see them so clearly. I sat in the dark in complete silence. The more I looked at those green lights the more I saw her in my mind. It happened all the time. Bethany was everywhere I looked, and if it wasn't something that reminded me of her then it was the yearning to want her beside me as I explored this land.

Iceland was a land of breathtaking contrasts, where fiery volcanoes rose next to glacial ice, and cascading waterfalls tumbled into serene lakes. Its rugged landscapes, adorned with black sand beaches, moss-covered lava fields, and the ethereal dance of the Northern Lights, created a visual symphony that captivated the soul. The beauty of Iceland was raw and majestic, a canvas painted by the forces of nature, evoking wonder and reverence with every vista. Yet, even in the shadow of such grandeur, my love stood apart. Bethany's beauty was not defined by towering peaks or shimmering glaciers; it radiated from a deeper place. It was in the warmth of her smile, the kindness in her gaze, and the laughter that filled the air when she was near. While Iceland's sights were breathtaking, they were a fleeting experience, a moment captured in time. Iceland might boast of nature's magnificence, but my heart knew that true beauty lay in the connection, the shared moments, and the depth of emotion that my love embodied for Bethany . Her beauty was not just seen but felt, a profound resonance that lingered long after the sights had faded from view. So, while Iceland enchanted the eye, it was Bethany who captured the heart, reminding me that beauty could be both grand and intimate, and that my soul's true landscape was shaped by my love for her.

Shaking my head to try and get the vision of her out of my mind, I got to my feet and headed inside. The apartment felt cold from the lack of personalization compared to my place back home in Chicago. I didn't have it in me, I just didn't care. Undressing myself as I headed into the shower, my skin tingled as images of a naked Bethany in my bed flashed in my mind. By the time I was in the shower, my dick was as hard as a rock. The hot water flowed down my back as I leaned on the wall with one hand while the other was placed on my shaft. Closing my eyes, I envisioned those emerald eyes, blond hair, and perfect naked body tied up. Those long legs spread open showcasing her pussy. Stroking my shaft as water poured over me, I envisioned exactly what I would do to her. So vivid in my mind, my heart began to beat faster and the head of my dick became increasingly sensitive. Picturing her body twitching beneath me and her cries of pleasure, a tingling sensation through my body became more intense until the contractions inside my cock pushed my semen toward the head. Right as I ejaculated, I heard Bethany's orgasm ring through my ears as if it were actually happening causing me to let out a cry of my own.

My mind went blank as I rested my head on the wall in front of me, giving me a sense of relaxation and calmness before I came to my senses and opened my eyes to see I was alone in the shower with my limp dick in my hand and my cum all over the wall. I laughed to myself thinking how different my life had become and whether it was worth it to continue living. No job, no woman, no status. I was a nobody – something I thought would never happen again.

Getting out of the shower, I wrapped a towel around my waist and lay in bed staring at the ceiling as my mind rewinded to the men who saved my ass 3 months ago. It bothered me I couldn't figure out who they were and how they were able to execute their plan of taking me. It dawned on me at the airport when I was walking to my gate that those men knew I'd be in that car and knew they were saving me. How would they know that? Why would they know that? And what did they want with me? Whatever those reasons were, I wasn't going to be a pawn in someone's game. My goal was to stay alive and figure out how to reunite with my sister safely.

But even a puzzle like that wasn't enough to distract my mind for long from Bethany. I had gotten myself a burner phone of my own while here just as a precaution. I grabbed it from the dresser beside me and stared at it. I knew it was wrong and the likelihood of getting caught was high but fuck it. Things couldn't get worse than they were now. Before being able to talk myself out of it, I already dialed the number and when I heard the sound of her voice, my body tingled.

"Hello."

"Happy birthday sweetheart."

Chapter Six

Bethany POV

I opened my eyes and stared at the ceiling; another day to survive – ugh. I was still mourning the loss of a man I loved while the man I was married to had no idea. Turning on my side, I faced my husband who was peacefully asleep. How little he knew about what had been going on the last three months. Since my brother killed Emilio, my depression had gotten so bad I'd been put on suicide watch. My own husband, who thought it was due to failed pregnancy attempts, agreed with my brother that someone should be with me at all times.

As I watched Pio slowly wake up, I put on a fake smile.

"Morning," he said. Pulling me into a cuddle as he rolled on top of me. His morning cock as stiff as ever placed in between my legs. "Happy birthday."

Right. Happy birthday to me. He kissed my neck as I remained still, mentally cringing at his touch. Pio was a good-looking man, but he wasn't Emilio. From the beginning of our arrangement, I'd learned to not pull away from his touch or to appear grossed out when he wanted to be intimate.

I felt him pull up my silk cami as his hands roamed my body. Eventually, he used one hand to pull his erection out of his boxers and then one of his fingers to move my panties out of the way so that the tip of his cock could rub against my opening. The only thing getting me through it was picturing him being Emilio. Closing my eyes, I pictured one of the many moments Emilio sent waves of pleasure through my body so that I was ready to receive my husband.

One minute and 10 seconds of happiness. As good as it was, whenever I'd open my eyes and see Pio instead of Emilio, the sadness flooded back in as it always did making me feel worse.

Pio rolled off me and got out of bed. "How did you sleep?"

"Better," I lied sitting up, throwing the Egyptian cotton sheets off of me.

"Are you sure you'll be okay with me gone for a few days?"

Nodding my head, "I will."

"You should stay with your mother while I'm gone."

I follow Pio into the master bathroom.

"I'll be fine," I assured him.

He gave me a worried look as he removed his boxers and turned on the shower. "I'd feel better knowing you had company while I was away."

I crossed my arms, "You never worried about me being lonely before."

Pio took a deep breath, "Well, I worry now."

"Pio..."

"Don't look at me like that Bethany."

"I promise I won't do anything stupid again."

"You promised me that 4 other times." The look of genuine concern on his face almost made me cry.

"I mean it this time."

"I wish I could believe that," his eyes darted to my arm.

His look pierced through the bandage around my forearm from my most recent self-inflicted wound last month. Suddenly, it felt like the skin under the bandage caught fire and I shook my arm as though it would make it stop.

"What is it going to take to earn your trust again?" I asked.

"When I know I can leave a knife, or pills, or alcohol out and not have to think about whether you'd use them to end your life." Pio stepped into the shower. "This is not up for discussion."

I couldn't argue with that. I'd put everyone that loved me in a position where they couldn't trust me anymore. The worst was having my own mother look at me with such disturbance. Whatever pain I was going through was nothing compared to my mother's pain as she watched me do horrible things to myself. She didn't deserve to see me like this, and I hated myself for being so weak.

Walking back into the bedroom, I collapsed back onto the bed. I needed to get my shit back together. What had I been doing the last 5 years aside from cheating on my husband with a man who was now dead. It was time to get over the pain of losing Emilio and rebuild myself. I lay there until Pio was out of the shower.

Sitting up when he entered the room, I blurt out, "I'm ready."

"Ready?" He asked with a confused face as I was still in my nightgown.

"I'm ready to stop mopping around. I'm ready to stop being a burden to everyone. I want to be back on my feet. Get back on track."

Walking over to me, he stood in between my legs and held my chin up to him. "Good. I'm happy to hear that." He placed a kiss on my forehead. "I'm sorry I have to miss your party tonight."

Giving a half smile, "It's okay."

It was not the first time I'd be attending an event without my husband but it hadn't bothered me before. Now that Emilio wasn't around, I'd really know what it was like to feel lonely amongst a crowd of people.

"I'll make it up to you," Pio said. Normally, I'd get gifts of diamonds or a fur coat as a sad attempt to make up for his lack of presence. "How about you and me go away for a while?"

"Away?" I repeated surprised. "Like a vacation?"

"A long vacation."

Now I was intrigued. Time away from here was what I desperately needed. "Where?"

Pio shrugged, "Maybe Europe? We can go wherever you want."

"Really? What about your duties?" I wasn't exactly sure what his role was in his family or under my brother but he traveled a lot – sometimes weeks at a time.

"I think we both need a getaway." Pio held my face in his hands and placed a kiss on my lips. "Think about it. When I get back this week, we will leave to wherever you choose."

"Okay," I replied. Pio turned around to head out of the bedroom and I found myself saying, "I'll be waiting for you."

He looked over his shoulder and shot me a warm smile and then walked out. Pio might not be the man I wanted but he was kind to me when I didn't even deserve it. Hopping off the bed, I got myself showered and dressed up for the day. Looking at myself in the mirror, it felt good seeing my hair brushed, makeup on, and in clothing other than an oversized T-shirt.

The doorbell rang just as I got to the bottom of the stairs. One of the maids opened the door and in flooded bouquets of flowers from my mother and sisters. As I was directing where to have them placed, Alfie appeared.

"Happy birthday old lady!" Alfie extended his arms and gave me a bear hug.

I lightly punched him as he let me go, "You aren't far behind."

"I'm not the one in their 30s," Alfie smirked. "I still have a few years."

"And when you turn 30, I'll make sure to remind you."

"I hope your gift is as good as mine," Alfie pulled out a box. Inside were the most breathtaking diamond earrings. The diamond was emerald and placed in the center of 4 gold leaves presented as a flower.

"Alfie," I breathed, "These are beautiful."

I walked over to the closest mirror on the wall, removed the gold hoops, and put on the ones Alfie gifted me. I could tell by the quality, weight, and size that these were pricey but that wasn't a problem for him now that he essentially took over Emilio's role and pay.

"Molly helped me pick them out," Alfie replied.

"You still talk to her?"

Alfie shrugged, "When I need some advice."

It stung hearing the hurt in his voice. Alfie always came to me for advice and I failed as a mentor the last few months.

"She has good taste," I smile.

Footsteps behind me sent chills up my spine. There was only one other male who would be allowed in this house. Unwilling to turn around, I locked eyes with Alfie who just looked past me and nodded. I watched Alfie walk away and leave me with the one person I despised.

"What are you doing here," my voice cold.

"I want to wish my little sister a happy birthday." Luca's calm demeanor felt insulting, I'd rather hear his cold tone toward me as it made it easier to stay angry with him.

I felt a tear slip down my face, "I don't have any brothers. They are both dead."

Walking out of the room, I closed myself in Pio's office and opened my purse to pull out tissues. It was my birthday and I wouldn't let Luca ruin it for me. The only time I had seen Luca the last three months was when I'd wake up in the hospital after one of my suicide attempts. He angered me. He was the reason behind all this and he knew it but the regret in his eyes wasn't enough to look past his actions – not this time.

Usually, Luca would push his way back into my good graces but he even understood he crossed a line he couldn't return from, so he let me be.

I sat on one of the leather chaise chairs breathing in and out. The inner rage was building up and blurring my mind. In the blink of an eye, I was at Pio's desk looking for anything sharp enough. By luck, I happened to lift the stapler to find a key to one of the locked draws that I knew held a gun. I was in a mental war with myself.

Open the drawer. Don't open the drawer.

Breathing in and out.

Open the drawer. Don't open the drawer.

Breathing in and out.

Open the drawer. Don't open the drawer.

Breathing in and out.

Eventually I dropped the key and placed it back under the stapler. Taking a deep breath, I then got to my feet and walked out of the room where I found Alfie leaning against the wall as though waiting for me while checking his phone. He looked up at me scanning my body to see if there was any harm.

"It hurts that you look at me differently."

"It's all in your head Bethany," Alfie commented as he remained relaxed.

"Is it?"

"You really want to argue on your birthday?"

"No," I replied.

"Then tell me what you'd like to do today."

"I need to pick up my dress and shoes for the party tonight, but I could do some shopping too."

Alfie had no issue driving me to different shops or carrying shopping bags as I had some retail therapy in addition to picking up my outfit for tonight. After getting my hair and makeup done, we headed back to my house so I could finish getting ready.

It was my grand 30th birthday party, and I needed a dress to match the occasion, so I opted to wear an Atelier Versace soft pink color gown. The form-fitting, cleavage-baring silhouette accented with a thigh-high slit and dramatic train was stunning; it gave an air of elegance under the amorousness. The top straps were able to hold up the girls as the dress hugged my waistline. The bottom of the dress had rosewater georgette enriched by delicate ruffle finishes, chantilly lace intarsia, and elegant micro material embroidery. I had last-minute custom-made platform heels to match the color of the dress and wore a diamond necklace that wrapped around my neck paired with my 3 carat diamond stud earrings.

"Pio is missing out," Alfie commented when he saw me.

Pio always seemed to miss out. "You wore the suit," I smiled in return.

Alfie didn't have the time to get something to wear tonight and if he was escorting me to my party, he needed to look the part. I had him get a navy color Armani suit with an accent tie to match my dress.

We arrived at the venue which was decorated from floor to ceiling in white and pink florals. It was an enchanted garden, the floor a white marble and the tables all clear glass. You'd think it was a redo of my wedding. Alfie and I walked in together but quickly parted our separate ways to entertain the various guests.

"Hot damn," Tiffany commented as I approached her and Natasha.

"You lost a ton of weight!" Natasha commented, "What's your secret?"

Death, I thought to myself but instead smiled and lied, "Extra Pilates classes."

"That's what you've been doing the last few months beside hiding from us?"

I couldn't have my two best friends see me a mess over a situation they didn't know about. As far as they were concerned, I was happily married.

"I need a drink," I stated.

We ordered a round of drinks and the girls caught me up on what was going on in their lives. As Natasha was speaking, her eyes widened and I knew someone was approaching us. I braced myself because the only person who would cause Natasha to stiffen like that aside from Emilio was Luca. Despite my hatred toward my brother, his invite was mandatory. As always, we had to appear as though we were in perfect harmony. Never dare show if there was a rift in the family, it would only get used against us.

Clearing his throat, "Ladies."

My body relaxed as I realized who it was and turned around. "Hamilton, you came."

Hamilton returned a warm smile and gave me a hug. "Happy Birthday Bethany. My father wasn't able to make it so I came in his place."

"Has it gotten worse?" I asked.

Hamilton nodded, "Doctor today said the cancer spread to his lungs. No coming back from there."

"I'm so sorry."

"Where's the husband?" Hamilton changed the subject.

We remained friends despite my arranged marriage. Hamilton understood without me having to explain myself as he too was bound for the same fate.

"Working, as always." I take a sip of my drink and realize both Natasha and Tiffany had walked away. "How's the wedding planning?"

"You mean how's paying everything that I have no say in? Expensive."

We both laughed but it quickly died out when a hand wearing a large emerald cut diamond engagement ring elegantly, set in a sleek platinum band, was placed on his chest as a reminder that this man was taken. The ring was a timeless piece that exuded sophistication and elegance. Words I wouldn't necessarily describe Kathy Harrington as.

"Bethany," Kathy smiled with such fake enthusiasm. "Happy birthday!"

"Thank you," I replied. "Hamilton was just talking about how excited he is for the wedding."

There was a sense of relief as she let out a breath and relaxed her shoulder. "Next month and I'll be Mrs. Branton. What a dream come true."

Hamilton wrapped his arm around her and pulled her into him. He was good at pretending but I saw right through this facade. This marriage stemmed from his father wanting to see him married before he passed.

"I'm happy for both of you."

Placing her hand on her chest, "I'm glad this hasn't ruined our friendship. You and Hamilton only had a brief entanglement but he assured me it wouldn't cause any tension."

Our friendship? I held back from laughing out loud. Kathy and I were more like frenemies. Neither one of us would bat an eye if we wanted to date the other's ex. As for the brief entanglement with Hamilton, I would just keep it at that.

"Hamilton and I were friends first," I replied, "And if both my friends are happy being together then who am I to get in between that."

Kathy [CJ4] wrinkled her nose and smiled as she knew I couldn't care less about her. Her dull auburn hair perfectly pinned up showcasing her pearl earring and necklace as I stood beside her; we looked like a contradiction – a mix between Audrey Hepburn and Marilyn Monroe.

"You'll be our first dinner guest after we move into the new house," Hamilton cocked a smile while Kathy rolled her eyes. He loved Kathy and I's so-called friendship, finding it amusing.

"We should go say hi to the mayor," she said.

"Luca DeCarlo just walked in," Hamilton said to her. "Let's go say hi to him first."

"Kissing ass already?" I commented.

"No," Hamilton said as though correcting me, "Just being polite."

"Sure," I laughed as I drank from my glass.

"Your brother requested a meeting," Kathy [CJ5] cut in as she always did when she felt the conversation was leaving her out.

"I didn't know that," I replied and shot Hamilton a look.

"Don't start. I'm not running for D.A." Hamilton said.

"Honey! You'd be amazing, " she encouraged.

"I agree, although I don't think you'd get along with Luca very well."

Hamilton laughed at my comment knowing exactly what I meant. "I'll catch you later." He took his fiancé's hand and they walk[CJ6]ed in the direction of my brother who was already looking at me. I turned away and looked for my friends who abandoned me for the dance floor.

"Thank you for that," I commented as I joined them.

"You let a good one go B," Natasha commented. "Too bad your brother didn't approve."

"Can we not talk about my brother? Not tonight – it's my birthday wish."

"Where's his wife?" Tiffany commented. "She should know better than to leave a good-looking man like him alone."

Before I could answer, the DJ cut the music. All focus turned to him as he spoke into the microphone.

"Ladies and gentlemen, let's give a round of applause to Bethany the birthday girl."

The crowd applauded me as I blew kisses in thanks.

"Bethany's big brother Luca has a few words."

I gulped as I watched Luca take the mic from the DJ. His stare bored into me, and it sent chills down my spine. It was like the calm before a storm except I didn't know what storm was coming. There was an uneasiness that disturbed me yet I didn't know where it stemmed from. It wasn't the usual look of pain in his eyes but one of fear.

"To my little sister, Bethany," Luca spoke so calmly. "May you always find happiness. To many more celebrations. Happy birthday." He raised his glass and everyone did the same as they cheered to me.

"Picture!" Isabelle screeched as she got us all together.

I stood in between my brother and mother with my sisters at both ends as we smiled at the camera. Flash. Flash. Flash. The more camera lights that went off the blinder I was getting. By the time I regained a clear vision, everyone had disbursed.

"Hey," Alfie came up behind me. "Gotta head out. Rosa said she'll take you home."

"Is everything okay?"

"Everything is fine. Just enjoy your party."

Before I could question him, Alfie was gone. He practically sprinted toward Luca and they both exited the venue.

The remainder of the night was fun, and I realized how much being around people helped lift my spirits – or maybe it was the alcohol. When I was dropped off at the empty house, all the lights were out except the one in the foyer. Part of me hoped I'd find someone there waiting for me other than a housemaid.

As I lay in bed staring up at the ceiling, I knew it was going to be another sleepless night. Getting out of bed, I walked to my dresser and dug out the burner phone that I used to communicate with Emilio. I kept it charged. There was one voicemail Emilio had left on there by accident. He had called the phone and it recorded him singing to a song in the car. I never told him about it but I was so happy to have kept it. On my worst days, I listen to it but I knew starting over that I would need to let it go.

Staring at the phone in my hand, I debated whether to get rid of it. Suddenly it rang, startling me. I dropped to the floor as a blocked number called it. The only person who knew the number was Emilio. My heart was beating out my chest as I reached for it. I was expecting a wrong number but when I heard his voice, I thought I had died and gone to heaven.

"Happy Birthday sweetheart."

Chapter Seven

I heard her gasp in realization then it went silent for a few seconds before Bethany spoke.

"You're alive," she whispered in almost a cry.

"I'm breathing if that's what you mean."

She began to silently sob, "I thought you were dead."

"I wasn't sure if you still had the burner phone but I just needed to hear your voice," I confessed. "I'm losing my mind over here."

"I miss you," Bethany sniffled.

"Everything okay over there?"

"It is now."

"Are you alone?"

"I'm alone. Pio is on a work trip."

"On your birthday?"

"It wouldn't be the first time. He threw me a big party to make up for it."

"Luca hasn't locked you up in a tower," I joked but my smile faded when Bethany went silent. "B? You there?"

"I never want to hear his name."

The vileness in her voice could cut the tension in the air. Sadly, it was evident that she had cut Luca out of her life for good.

"Then tell me what you want to hear."

"You," she replied, "I just want to hear you."

"I dream of you every night," I confessed.

"If this wasn't an old school burner phone then I could send you a picture."

"I guess you'll have to tell me."

"I'm in my mini pink silk night cami. The one you got me."

An image of her wearing it flashed into my mind. "With the heels?" I asked.

"Just the way you like. I wish you were here."

"I wish I was too. Have you pinned against the wall."

"Just pinned against the wall?" Bethany asked in a begging tone.

"You know damn well you'd be naked and I'd sucking on those beautiful tits of yours."

"Do you think about that often?"

"All the time." Lying in bed, I could feel the tingling sensation in my boxers. "What I'd give to get you on your knees with my cock deep in your throat."

"You know how to make a girl blush." Bethany giggled. "Close your eyes. Pretend I'm there."

My eyes shut and immediately the image of her naked body was in front of me.

"Go on," I urged.

"My wrists are tied to the ends of the headboard, my legs wide open for you, ready for your command."

I sharply inhale at the image. Then take charge just as she liked it.

"I want you to touch yourself in all the places I say."

"I'm ready." The excitement in Bethany's voice hyped me up even more.

"My tongue traces the curves of your body as I make my way up to your nipples. Swirling my tongue around one time, two times, then three times before I bite down on it."

I hear Bethany lightly inhale as she must be squeezing down on her nipple. "Keep going."

"My hand makes its way down to your pussy. Are you following baby?"

"Mhmm."

"Sucking on your nipple as I slide my middle finger up and down your clit."

My dick started throbbing. I didn't even have the ability to get into foreplay, I just wanted to dive in. Pulling my erection out, I slowly began touching myself, still keeping my eyes closed and imaging Bethany touching herself to my words.

"Up and down. Up and down. Now using my middle finger and ring finger, I do a slow circular motion."

"MMM," Bethany breathed into the phone.

"Now split both fingers one on each side of that clit and slide them up and down against the wall of your pussy. Are you getting wet baby?"

"Oh yeah."

"Picking up the pace just a little bit and don't stop until you're nice and wet," I instructed as I stroked my dick.

When a light moan escaped her lips, I went on. "Now slide the middle finger further down entering your pussy."

"How many fingers?" Bethany asked.

"Use all four for me. Slide them in and out each time going in deeper."

"I need you," Bethany panted. "I need you."

Her begging was electrifying. "Curl your fingers when you're inside, apply pressure against the wall."

When I heard her breathing pick up, so did my hand going up and down my shaft.

"Emilio," Bethany panted.

"Close your eyes baby. Imagine it's me throwing your legs over my shoulders."

Her moaning was sending me over the edge as my pre-ejaculation coated my dick for lubrication as I picked up the pace.

"Faster," I grunted.

Bethany was losing herself, I could hear it in her moaning.

Lost in my own imagination I busted at the sound of Bethany crying out in pleasure.

"Shit," I spat out watching my cum burst out of my dick and all over my hands.

It took us both a few seconds to relax.

"I didn't say to cum yet."

"I couldn't resist," Bethany replied.

There was rumbling in the background that startled Bethany. "I need to go. Call me tomorrow, same time."

Then there was a click. Standing there with cum all over me and alone sent a wave of frustration through my body. I hated being here. I hated this life. I hated I had to make a choice to continue this for the sake of living or go all out for one last moment of pleasure. My mind raced as I came up with a plan that seemed impossible to achieve.

After showering, I grabbed my phone and made a call I didn't want to make. It was risky but I was willing to gamble it all just to be able to touch Bethany again.

"Well look who is it. Crawling back now?"

"Get over yourself Athena," I sneered, "I need big a favor. No questions no comments – it's either yes or no."

There was a pause, "What can I do for you?"

Chapter Eight

It was too late to change my mind. I was already at the airport with my ticket in hand. I nodded as the TSA agent handed me back the passport. It never failed me how money could easily persuade people. I looked nothing like the man on the passport but the $100 bill the TSA agent found when he opened it disagreed. As I made my way through the bustling airport, the sounds of announcements and rolling suitcases were a chaotic backdrop to the whirlwind of emotion swirling within my heart. Glancing at the departure board, my heart continued to race as I scanned for my flight, and seeing each destination only made me wish I could be where I really wanted – in Bethany's arms.

As much as I wanted Bethany in my arms, this was a suicide mission that I was slowly talking myself out of. As I walked past the gates ready for flights to different places, an attendant caught my eye. Blond hair wrapped up in a bun helping a passenger with a question at the desk in front of the gate. She reminded me of Bethany and there was a powerful tug at my heart. Sometimes life threw you signs and you just needed to go with it.

Today felt nostalgic as my past seemed to play before my eyes.

"Rachel told her sister how you're a bit tight on cash," Marco says.

Uncomfortable that Rachel would say something like that, I shrug it off, "Times are a bit tough right now. Nothin' I can't handle."

"I've asked around about you. You keep your head down and out of trouble. Work 3 jobs to support your mother and sisters."

Now it is really uncomfortable. If he knows that much then he knows my mother is a junkie and my sisters don't share the same father as I do.

"I do what I can. What can I get ya to drink?" I say wiping down the bar countertop.

"a 7-7." Marco leans on the bar. "I got a job for you. Pays more than what you're making busting your ass 24 hours a day."

Marco is a made-man and I know what kind of work he needs done.

"It's not my style," I politely decline.

"I only ask once," he looks at me gravely. "$2,000 for a job doesn't sound too bad, does it? All cash."

With widened eyes, I hand him his drink. 2k for one job. That will go a long way.

"Think about it. If you're interested meet at the pond when the sun sets tomorrow." Marco walks away with his drink and goes to a table where 2 other men are seated.

I had no intention of going. It was thundering outside and the night sky lit up with bolts of lightning as I walked home, barely being able to see in front of me. Home. Most people find home their safe haven but for me – it was the last place I'd rather be. The only thing that kept me from getting my own place was my two sisters. Cassie and Marie weren't old enough to fend for themselves. I was the reason they had food to eat, clean clothes to wear, and a roof over their heads. Finally reaching the front of the broken down house, I huffed in frustration at the loud music. Typical behavior from my mother. She was having one of her parties and I was surprised the cops hadn't shown up yet.

A few people were in front of the house chatting barely able to stand up.

"Party's over," I say to them sternly.

"Buzz kill!" one of them said.

"That's Cindy's son. Hates when she gets to have a little fun," the other sneers at me.

Choosing to ignore them, I entered the house. The music got louder when I opened the door and the house was covered in smoke. Tobacco smoke, cannabis smoke, bong smoke – you name it. People making out, people passed out drunk, people dancing. It was a mess.

"Parties over!" I shout as I turn off the music. "Get the fuck outta here."

Quickly searching the house for my lack of a mother, I find her in the kitchen cooking up some meth. Nothing pisses me off more than her doing stupid shit in the house.

"Everyone out!" I shout.

"E," my mother slurs her words, "I thought you were at work."

"Yeah, that was hours ago." I turn off the stove and again tell everyone to leave, "You don't need to go but you need to get the fuck outta here."

Everyone in the kitchen moans in disagreement making my mother protest. "This isn't your house E. If anything, I should be telling you to leave."

Tired and angry, I get in her face, "If you don't cut this party – I'll call the cops right now."

She sneers, "You rat!" lunging at me, I move aside and watch as she falls to the floor.

Sick to my stomach, I walk toward the staircase to my sisters bedrooms to check on them. Both of them are in my tiny bedroom crunched up in bed. Cassie is awake holding Marie in her arms.

"Hey," she whispers when she sees me enter the room. "E, we can't." Dried tears on her face let me know she was up all night consoling Marie. They hate nights like these.

"I know," I reply. "Gonna make some changes around here. Promise."

There is no other choice. I need get them out of here and Marco is the answer.

The flight was just under 4 hours but within that time all I could think about was my past. It felt like I fell from the top and am now worse than I was before I became Emilio Pugliese. If only I were back in the simpler times when I was just E.

"Why me?" I stand looking confused.

"You knew my brother, Marco."

"Knew him on the streets, did a favor or two but I wouldn't call him a friend."

"We were talking just moments before he was killed," Luca gulps and clears his throat, "He told me if I ever needed help or didn't know who to trust that without question it'd be you."

I inhaled and exhaled as the plane took off the ground causing flutters in my stomach.

"I'm not one of you." I know how things work in this lifestyle, you can only be initiated into the family if you are of Italian blood. "It's code and you're breakin' it."

"I'm about to break more than just a code," Luca shoots back. "Who will know anyway?"

"The fellas here, in Chicago, to start."

"Who says we are staying in Chicago?" Luca is confident, almost making me believe I can pull it off. "You just need a name that sounds Italian. What does E stand for?"

"It's just E."

"Your mother just picked a letter?"

"Inspired by one of her favorite party candy." It is the first time divulging that to anyone but it is true.

Luca, taken back by everything about me, nods his head. "Okay, so pick a name that starts with E. Introduce yourself as that name and let everyone start calling you that."

"No one close to me is going to go for that."

"When they know who you work for they will."

"You're not taking no for an answer are you?" I shake my head, "No one will take you seriously having me as your right hand."

"No one knows enough about you to know the facts," Luca pulls out a carton of cigarettes and hands one to me.

I knew if I took one that I'd be committing to his plan and serving as his right hand - this would be life changing. Cassie and Marie would be taken care of. Cassie can open up the beauty salon she always wanted, and Marie can go to a better school. Extending my hand, I took the cigarette.

"Snack? Drink?" The stewardess snapped me out of my thoughts.

"You got something strong? Pour me whatever you got."

Handing me a cup of brown liquor, I took a sip. The person sitting next to me was tapping his finger on the tiny tray in front of him.

"Itching for a smoke?" I mention.

"These nicotine patches are trash."

The grumpy response made me laugh.

"I used to loathe people who smoke," the man went on, "and now it's the only thing that calms me down."

"What got you started?"

"Work."

With a smile, "It's always work."

Chapter Nine

I leaned my head back into the chair. As the plane soared high above the clouds, my fingers twitched with an urgency I could hardly ignore. The familiar craving for a cigarette gnawed at me, a relentless reminder of my last indulgence before boarding. I glanced around at the rows of passengers, each absorbed in their own world, blissfully unaware of the battle waging within my soul. The tiny, cramped cabin felt suffocating, each breath a stark reminder of my confinement, and the no-smoking sign glaring above me like a cruel taunt. The metallic taste of anxiety lingered in my mouth, mingling with the hum of the engines. I closed my eyes, desperately willing the urge to subside. It was a test of willpower in the most unlikely of places, and as the miles stretched beneath them, I found myself counting down the minutes until I could finally step onto solid ground and light up once more. The only other craving that would satisfy me was Bethany's touch.

I hadn't taken up smoking until I was in my 20s – it was a reminder of who I became. It flashed me back to the moment that put my name on everyone's radar and my own addiction to smoking.

"The Gustos are out."

"Fuck!" Luca slams his glass of liquor onto the floor. "If we don't secure this territory, we are done." He has become good at masking his Chicago accent; however, right now, he comes out full force due to his anger.

"We can make a peace deal," I suggest.

"NO," Luca raises his voice. "We didn't come to California to fucking make deals for peace or get stepped all over. If we want to be able to take over Chicago, we need the resources to do so. This is our opportunity to make a name and gain some traction."

He is right. Luca has a plan of action to take over Chicago from the Baricelli family, however before we could go back to our city to claim it, so it is crucial we have the money and power to do so first. Around here the Razzano Family had the connections to everything.

"The other families want to be allies but they can't commit," I explain to Luca. "They are scared to go against the Razzano family and rightfully so. The last family to go against them barely made a wave before they were all lynched on display in front of their own homes."

"So make a statement," Luca looks at me with just pure evil in his eyes. "Go meet with Roberto Razzano and don't you leave until we have the upper hand."

With a nod of my head, I turned on my heels and walked away. I spent the night thinking about what to say or even how to tell the most powerful family in California to step down from overtaking our area. We spent a year claiming this area – and Luca wasn't going to give it up easily.

How do you take power away from someone? You kill their reputation – although everyone was too scared to go against them so that wasn't working. You kill the head of the family – that would only bring us heat and it was not something we could handle alone at the moment. There was only one other option left. You stop their cash flow – no money means no way to fund your resources; no one did anything for free.

This would be without a doubt the biggest accomplishment in my role as Consigliere to Luca. Just as this was important to Luca – it was important to me for a different reason. I wasn't Italian – it didn't make me less of a person but unless you are Italian you weren't ever viewed as one of them. You could dabble in the lifestyle but you could never be inducted in. Truth be told I didn't know what I was. My mother claimed I was a bit of everything but she was a junkie so that meant shit. Luca was crazy to have me as his Consigliere and no one took him seriously because of it. I was the exception to the rule for him – which was why I needed to make people fear my name if they wouldn't respect it.

It took a week for Roberto Razzano, the head of the family, to meet with me at his vineyard. This place was a gold mine. Without needing to take shares from other family's revenue, he would still be able to survive off this place alone. He had a table set up on the terrace balcony overlooking the vineyard but only his seat had a plate setting in which he was eating Pappardelle Bolognese in a deep porcelain plate. The smell of the red sauce made my mouth water. A woman came out and sprinkled parmigiano cheese over the pasta. Roberto watched me watch her do it. He must think I was starving for a bite, meanwhile I was just checking out the girl's ass. She made it look like art as she held the large spoon over the pasta and lightly let it fall into the dish.

"April here is the best cook on the East Coast. Will cook anything I want whenever I want," Roberto says as the woman walks away.

With a fork in one hand and a spoon in another, Roberto twirled pasta using the utensils so that it neatly wrapped around the fork and could easily be put into his mouth. He looked at me observing my reaction. He wanted me to feel like a starving dog watching his master eat. It made me hate the man even more.

"Next time ask for a salad," I say looking at the buttons of his shirt that look like they are about to burst.

Holding back a sneer, he replies with his mouth full, "Pasta is the heart and soul of a true Italian."

He was insulting me now, yet I remained calm as thoughts of ripping his throat out played in my mind.

"I'll make sure my wife is Italian who will cook for me all the time. That way I know what it's like not be able to look at my dick."

This pisses him off. "Better to know you have one then not." The two men behind him looked like pit bulls ready to attack at his command.

His threat to chop mine off should have scared me but it only fueled the fire. "This is the last chance at backing down peacefully."

Roberto laughs, "If Luca wants to dig his own grave, then I'll let him."

"He'd rather not start any problems."

Scooping another bite of pasta into his mouth, "Tell Luca, from me to him – fuck off. You Chicago men think you're so tough coming here and take what's mine." He waves his fork at me as though that will dismiss me from the table. When I don't budge, he goes on, "Do you want your sister to find you with your brains blown out? My men will make it look like a suicide."

Now he struck a nerve. Whether he knew about my little sister Marie committing suicide that same way or not, negotiations were now off the table. Getting to my feet, I straightened my suit jacket.

"It was a pleasure," I smile. Taking out a cigarette, I show myself out.

As I walked toward the car, a plane flew overhead. I got into the vehicle just in time. The smell of gasoline filled the air. I heard commotion happen as someone yelled when they realized the plane wasn't spraying pesticides over the grape vines. Puffing on the cigarette, I smoke it right until I get to the gate and before I turn onto the road, I toss the cigarette out the window and onto the lawn. It caught fire immediately and within minutes, the vineyard was destroyed.

That was the downfall of Roberto Razzano, the rise of Luca DeCarlo, and the respect I got as Consigliere.

Fuck it. Unbuckling my seatbelt, I got up heading to the bathroom. Two flight attendants were cleaning up the cockpit area but looked up and smiled at me.

"Is everything okay?" One of them asked.

"About to be," I winked shooting her a smile that made her swoon so that she wouldn't notice I swiped a knife from one of the carts from first class. "If you could get me a soda, I'd appreciate it. I'm at seat 28C.

"Of course," she smiled.

"Thank you darling," I replied as I opened the bathroom door, slid in, and securely locked myself in.

The cramped bathroom of the airplane was dimly lit, the faint hum of the engines providing a low, rhythmic vibration unfolding within its tiny confines. I turned my attention to the small, smoke detector located within the wall looming above me. With eagerness, I popped out the detector from the ceiling using the knife. With the thin head of the dull knife, I slowly and carefully unscrewed the pin holding the face of the detector. Once I removed the top, I ripped out the detector piece dismantling it all together.

A rush of adrenaline coursed through me as I pulled out a small tin that held my cigarettes and a lighter. As I lit the cigarette, the soft glow of the ember cast fleeting shadows on the cramped walls. The first drag filled my lungs with a sharp release, the smoke curling upward, dissipating into the stale air. With each inhale, I closed my eyes, letting the memory of Bethany wash over me like a warm wave. I could hear her laughter, a sweet melody that had once filled my world with light replacing the need for this addiction.

In that moment, as the smoke spiraled into the air, and I was transported back to that night on the beach, where the salty breeze had mingled with the scent of her shampoo.

Under the cloak of night, the moon cast a silvery glow upon the tranquil waves, creating a shimmering path that led directly to the secluded stretch of beach where I found Bethany looking out toward the ocean. Taking one more look behind me toward the hotel making sure no one had followed me, I let out a sigh of relief. Bethany turned around to face me, her long blond hair blown to the side as she smiled, standing there in a thin white short night gown. She looked like an angel, and I the devil she so eagerly was waiting for.

"You sure no one saw you leave the room?" I question as I approach her.

"Everyone is asleep. I snuck out of the room from my terrace." Bethany smirks at her choice of booking a ground floor room.

Holding her face with my hand, I pulled her in for a kiss. My other hand placed on the small of her back, I felt every part of her body against mine. The cool, damp sand, and the air was thick with the scent of salt water, the soft sound of the ocean lapping against the shore wrapped us in a world neither one of us wanted to escape. As our lips parted, we both leaned our foreheads forward as they rested on one another.

"Please tell me you have something up your sleeve for tomorrow."

"Not this time sweetheart."

"How am I supposed to lay in bed with him every night?" Bethany's voice is soft as she spoke.

"I'm sorry," is all I could say.

Staring into each other's eyes, we found solace in each other, creating a memory that would linger long after the tides washed away our footprints in the sand.

"He'll want kids."

The lump in my throat makes it hard to speak, "So you will give that to him."

"I want them to be yours."

I place a kiss on her forehead. "You have to play the role Bethany. He can't suspect a thing."

Her emerald eyes hold back tears. "If this is the only way I can still have you – then I will do it."

"I love you."

I'd never said those words to a woman before and it was the first time confessing it to Bethany. It was the night before her marriage to Pio, so I was shitty on timing but I had to say it. She had to know how much of a struggle this was for me just as it was for her. Bethany's eyes sparkled like the stars above, reflecting the emotions that danced between us—desire, excitement, and a hint of trepidation as our breaths mingled in the warm night air.

I led her onto the ledge of rocks that piled out into the water where waves crashed into them. Sitting on the edge, Bethany swung her leg over straddling me. The heat coming off her body warmed my skin. She felt like home. Our lips touched and we fell into a deep passionate kiss. My hands wondered up her thin night gown and it was no surprise she was wearing nothing underneath. Bethany slowly rocked her hips as our tongues massaged one another. My dick hardened from the heat and feel of her rubbing against it. Reaching into my sweatpants, I pulled it out guiding it to her entrance. Bethany raised herself and then gently lowered herself onto the tip until I was fully inside of her. She paused a moment allowing the walls of her pussy to tighten around my cock as she placed her mouth back onto mine. Slowly, she rocked her hips forward and back, from time to time she pulled out of our kiss to catch her breath. Neither one of us ready for this to end. When I felt her walls tighten, I knew she was approaching her climax. Holding out from my own orgasm, I waited for her to finish first – just like I always have. Her breathing got heavier, her hands gripped my shoulders for support, her muscles began to stiffen as her body prepared for its release while I watched this beautiful women give herself to me. The waves aggressively crashed into the rocks adding intensity to the sensual intimate moment.

"I'm going to cum," she moans.

She looked to me for permission and I nod my head. We both climax. Thankfully we were far enough not to be heard.

I let out a grunt, semen spilling into the toilet. Reality crept back in and I was back in the sterile confines of the airplane bathroom with my dick in hand and a cigarette in my mouth. Cleaning myself up I had to laugh at the current situation. Each drag of the cigarette was bittersweet, a fleeting tribute to a love that felt both achingly present and impossibly distant.

I, Emilio Pugliese, am in love with a woman I cannot have.

Chapter Ten

Bethany POV

The water from my new showerhead poured down heavy so that it felt as though you were standing under a waterfall. As I submerged my entire body under the water with shut eyes, I reached out to my cherry blossom body wash and pumped some into my hand to lather onto my body. Sounds of water splattering on the floor while lost in thought, I rinsed off all the body wash from my skin. Luca must know Emilio is alive. It would make sense why there was no funeral and no word about Emilio being removed from his position. I thought it was just so no one would know there was such betrayal in the family. Since I wasn't allowed to speak Emilio's name, there was no way for me to know for sure.

I turned the knob cutting off the flow of water. Squeezing the excess water from my hair before stepping out of the shower, I didn't even bother wrapping a towel around me. My phone conversation with Emilio put me in a good mood and I couldn't stop smiling. It was all going well until I was interrupted by Alfie who came to let me know the house would be under tight surveillance the next few weeks.

While brushing my hair, I made my way toward the phone placed on the dresser charging.

"Now that's a sight," a man's voice said behind me, causing me to scream in fear.

I turned around to see a figure standing in my room, the light from the master bathroom wasn't enough to show me his face. Naked, I stood there trembling. As he stepped forward, a beam of light hit his face, and when I saw the scar over his left brow, I gasped. Is this real? Am I dreaming? I stood there in shock.

"I just couldn't –"

Before he even finished, I jumped into his arms pulling his head toward mine so I could finally taste him again. I didn't care how he made it here but he wasn't leaving this room. Refusing to unlock my lips from his even when I barely had oxygen to breathe, there was this urge to feel even closer to him. Clinging onto this shoulder, I hoisted myself up and wrapped my legs around his waist in which he grabbed onto my thighs. I missed everything about him. His scent, his touch, his lips, his hands...everything.

"Bethany, are you okay?!" I hear Alfie on the other side of my bedroom door trying to open it.

Unlocking my lips from his, I reply, "I'm fine, just stubbed my toe." Before slamming my mouth back onto his, I looked at Emilio, "You re-membered to lock the door."

Shooting me a smirk, we were back at it. I melted under the warmth of his mouth. Emilio made his way to the bed and fell onto it with him on top. I pulled his shirt off as he undid his pants while we both refused to break our mouths apart. Emilio raised himself up to his knees to pull his shirt over his head and pull his pants down to his knees before hovering back over me.

"You're gonna have to keep quiet," Emilio quietly said to me.

"I don't care if this whole damn house hears me scream your name."

"As much as I want to hear it, I don't want any interruptions."

"No promises. I want to feel you inside of me. Taste all of you." Grabbing his hair, I pulled his head up and made eye contact. "I want your dick so far down my throat that I choke on it."

His eyes sparkled at hearing my words. Emilio loved when I spoke to him like that but the act itself I knew he loved. The feel of him on me was sending bolts of electricity through me.

"You don't miss fucking my mouth?" I went on.

The feel of his cock twitched so hard against my thigh it made me giggle.

"You're asking for it," he breathed against my skin.

"Whenever. However. Wherever."

Emilio positioned himself so that his hip was over my face and his erect dick up against the side of my ear. Without needing to say a word, I opened my mouth wide and directed his erection into my mouth. The sound of him holding back a growl as he sunk his hips onto my face with his dick fully inserted into my mouth. My mouth salivated as I wrapped my tongue around it and breathed through my nose. My arms wrapped around his thighs and my hands grabbed his plump ass. I missed digging my nails into his flesh.

EMILIO POV

Bethany glanced up to me. She was eager, just as I am, and wasn't looking for any further delay. Watching as my erection slid into her mouth, I let out a pant. The warmth of her mouth around my cock, her tongue immediately wrapping around it had my leg shaking from excitement. Bethany wrapped her arms around my thighs and her hands grabbed my ass. She wasn't kidding about not holding back. Who am I to deny her wishes? It wasn't long before my entire length vanished into her mouth and down her warm, wet throat.

I held my hips to her face and started thrusting my hips. Her head was pinned in between the bed and my hips, there was no way for her to escape.

Her hands squeezed my ass to confirm she was okay and to keep going. It didn't take me long to lose control as I fucked her mouth so violently she could have easily suffocated, but not my girl. My girl was able and willing to take it all. I could feel her throat wrapped around my cock, ready to milk it of all the cum it had to offer. She drank my cum like her life depended on it. When it was over, I lay beside her as my mind felt as though it exploded.

"Are you okay?" I asked once my mind and body settled down.

"Never been better," Bethany smiled as she lay there covered in a mixture of her saliva, sweat, and my cum. "Don't tell me you're done already."

I couldn't help but smirk. My plan was to take all of her before attempting to get out of here. Surprisingly, the house was fully guarded, thankfully, the secret pathway was clear up until reaching the hallway to the bedroom. Getting out was going to be tricky, and I didn't have high hopes of succeeding. Despite that, I didn't regret this – not one bit. Turning onto my side, I reached for her to do the same so that we were laying side by side. How am I going to go another day without her?

"What are you thinking about?" Bethany asked.

"Nothing," I replied truthfully. I was inhaling this moment for as long as possible.

There was a change in her eyes as though she came to a realization that our time was limited. "Take me with you."

Taking her hand, I kissed her palm. "I'll be lucky if I make it out of here myself." Glancing down her arm, I noticed the bandage. "What happened?" Being so caught up in seeing her how did I not notice her arm?

Bethany pulled away. "I accidentally hurt myself. I'm okay."

Bethany POV

"Accidentally?" Emilio's eyebrows were scrunched together and the area around his mouth tightened.

"I'm fine," I assured him.

"Did Pio do something to you?"

"No. I was cutting up in the kitchen and I was clumsy."

His face became even more demure. His knuckles turned white from clenching his fists. The pain was written all over his face. Suddenly I felt embarrassed. Self-harming was my way of acting out but now being in front of Emilio it felt childish and selfish of me. His sister took her own life – something he rarely spoke about but I knew it haunted him still to this day. Emilio would always hold it over himself that he could have prevented it if he had only been around more. So with my mistake staring at him in the face, I couldn't admit to it.

"Bethany," his voice was soft with a frustrated tone as he got off the bed walking to the other side of the room.

Emilio POV

How could she? All I could see was blood, everywhere. A lump in my throat made it hard to speak.

"Marie! I'm home," shouting as I walk through the house.

My mother was passed out on the sofa probably fresh from coming home from a night of binging. Cassie called for me to come to the house and have a pep talk with Marie about things that were going on at school. Working for Luca had made it possible to put Marie into a good school, giving her a shot out of this neighborhood; however, it hadn't been easy for her. She was a good kid and smart, but she had the attitude of a hood girl and that wasn't meshing well with her stuck up classmates.

"Marie! Where the hell are you?" I make my way upstairs.

By step three, I got an eerie feeling that I couldn't shake off. Maybe it was due to not being here for a few days at a time but I was actively working with Luca on setting his plan in motion to take over the city. When I got to the top of the stairs, I saw the door to the bathroom shut. Walking past it, I got an odd chill up my spine. First I checked her bedroom where she normally was to avoid being around our mother. Nothing. I checked Cassie's room, where she liked to use her makeup and wear her clothes. Nothing. When Marie felt scared or lonely, she would stay in my room which didn't seem likely since the last time we spoke it was an argument. She hated her school but hated it more that I wasn't around as much. I told her I'd make it up to her and she seemed to lighten up. She even called me this morning and told me that she was grateful to have me – I'd be a liar if I said it didn't warm my heart. Cassie and I raised her like she was our child protecting her from as much as possible being exposed to a junkie mother like ours. When I didn't see her in my room, I felt nauseous. Where was she? This bad feeling only got stronger and instinctively I was avoiding going into the bathroom, but there was no other place to check. Maybe she was out with the new friend she made, at this point I'd even allow her to go out with the boy she was crushing on. The closer I got to the door, there was a weight on me as though slowing my motion. The chill went down my spine again when I touched the doorknob.

"Marie? You in there?"

Silence. I smelled it. That awful scent of metal. The lump in my throat seemed to start cutting off my oxygen flow knowing exactly what that thick aroma was. Marie what did you do? Opening the door, I opened a life full of trauma.

"E, what do you want for dinner?" Cassie shouts but her voice is so faint.

I felt her behind me and then a screeching sound at the sight before our eyes.

"I'm sorry," Bethany's voice was low and the shame in her tone sent a pang to my heart.

"I'm the one who should be apologizing." Walking over to her, I placed a kiss on her forehead. If I had just kept my dick in my pants from the start she wouldn't be in this situation.

Looking into my eyes, she grazed my face. Her finger slowly traced the scar over on my brow. Deep down I knew she would try to take her own life but somewhere inside me held hope she wouldn't do such a thing.

"I've been struggling the last few months," Bethany's confession was the most genuine I've heard from her, "I thought you were dead and it felt as though I died too. Part of this was to make Luca feel the guilt of taking your life. It was worth seeing the look on his face every time, but if I could take it back I would."

Her voice cracked and displayed in her green eyes was a deep shame. I dragged my hand up to her hip and clamped my grip lightly pressing my thumb into her. The breath she was holding spilled, though she didn't move a muscle.

"Give me your word you won't do it again," I commanded, flexing my hand just a fraction so it tightened my grip on her hip.

"You have my word," she sucked in a breath of air.

I held her, locked in a stare of anticipation for a few moments before slamming my mouth to hers and walking us to the nearest wall. My ability to distract her from some of her misery was all I had and I'd use it with no remorse or hesitation. The feel of her large breasts squished against my hard chest, every curve she had melting into every sharp muscle on me ramped up my need to be inside of her.

With a house full of guards, it didn't stop me attacking her lips with force, allowing her to devour me just as I was devouring her. I missed the feel of her fingernails ravaging my shoulders and back, her whimpers of pleasure sinking into my brain and making my head spin with desire.

I bit on her lip and tugged back until it popped free of my teeth. "Not a sound out of you."

Chapter Eleven

I panted and rested my lips on her again, our tongues dancing feverishly as I lifted her and took her to the bed. The cool satin of the sheets was a welcome sensation across our hot bodies. Getting up on my knees, I spread her legs wide open and took a moment to look at that beautiful cunt. I was barely touching her but she was glistening in the dim room. Taking my cock, I slapped her clit with it a few times before I was ready to go again. Placing the tip of my cock at her entrance, I slid it up and down making her wetter and using her juices as a lubricant. Her body was already squirming.

"Fuck me already," Bethany begged.

Taking her legs, I placed one on each shoulder. Slowly pushing my hips forward, her eyes widened as my cock filled her up. I couldn't risk her not making a sound, so I placed one hand on her throat, my fingers wrapping around her neck. Raising my thumb so that they were pressing against the area one inch below her chin where I could feel the bottom of her tongue in her mouth. Pushing up toward the throat, I could see that her breathing was becoming more difficult but not impossible.

"Focus on me baby."

She nodded her head as I held my grip and slowly thrust in and out of her. It was a win-win. This would ensure no marks would be left behind while she could get off without us getting caught. My other hand's fingers dug into the back of her thighs, lifting her higher, so I could get more leverage. I knew she was enjoying herself as her eyes rolled back and she pushed her hips up into mine. She was about to lose it.

"Not yet," I commanded needing to enjoy this a little longer.

The feel of her neck tensed as she opened her mouth to try and breathe. Falling on top of her as I was grinding firmly, retreating slowly and flowing back controlling my own orgasm from exploding. I dug my face into the crook of her neck to suppress my own cries of pleasure as her body was attacked by feverish spasms under me.

"Now," I said once I felt the point of no return, I began slamming my hip forward repeatedly.

Loosening my grip while drawing back and striking precisely one last time, she filled her lungs with air as her body exploded with an intense yet silent orgasm while my own followed after. I collapsed on top of her as she tried to regain her breath.

"Learned something new while away?"

"Something I wanted to try." I wasn't sure if her comment was a trick question so I changed the subject. "What's going on with all the security here?"

Bethany rolled her eyes. "That night you called and I had to rush off the phone, Alfie said the house was going to have a few more guards. I figured since Pio was gone it was just a precaution."

"Makes sense," I agreed, but knew it had to be more. There weren't just a few guards around because her husband was away. Something was going on. Checking the time on the clock on the nightstand, I jumped out of bed. "I need to go."

"Emilio...." Bethany hopped off the bed. "Is this the last time I will see you?"

Without answering her, I gave her a look which caused her eyes to water.

"It is," I whispered as I began getting dressed. I placed a kiss on her forehead then finished putting on my clothes. Bethany grabbed a robe to put on herself.

"I'll make sure the hallway is cleared," she said.

My heart was beating out my chest from nervousness. If I made it out the house, I'd be lucky, and to make it back out of the country would be a miracle. Standing against the wall beside the door, I watched Bethany slide open the French doors to her bedroom and check the hallway. Entering back in, she nodded her head.

"It's clear."

The look of disappointment on her face brought a tone of sadness. She saw it in my eyes and understood this would be the last time we would see one another again.

"You have a whole life ahead of you. Don't let it go to waste."

She nodded her head. "I'll always love you. I'm just happy you're alive." Walking up to me, she placed a soft kiss on my lips. "You take your own advice, will you – go and be happy, for me."

I embraced her one last time, letting our tongues dance with one another while inhaling her scent before I left for good. Pulling away before I changed my mind, I stepped back and took one last look before I slid out the room and dashed down the hall. Each quick step sent a blow to my heart. The morning sunrays cast a yellow tone glow through the windows illuminating the delicate lace curtains. The secret pathway entrance was hidden in plain sight. If you knew which lamp had the button to make a small portion of the wall in the hallway slide allowing you down the pathway then you could enter and exit the house from a block away.

Approaching the lamp, the taste of freedom was just a few steps away; however, before I even lifted my hand to the lamp, I heard my name.

"Emilio."

A jolt of paralyzation shot through my body. Finding it hard to move my stiff muscles, I managed to turn around.

"Grace," I replied stoically.

"Alfie said you were away on business in Europe and things went south," she lowered her voice as she got closer to me, "We thought you were dead."

"You thought wrong."

"How long have you been around?"

"Doesn't matter, I need to get out of here."

Grace looked at me unsure of what to do. "You're in hiding from the DeCarlos."

I exhaled a deep breath, avoiding her question, "You're holding me up."

"If you came for her," Grace nodded in the direction of Bethany's room. "You're better off taking her."

Furrowing my brows, "What for?"

"The girl is on suicide watch. Why do you think I'm up here?"

That lump in my throat was back and Grace's words had me worried that Bethany had no reason to stop harming herself if this was going to be our last encounter.

"And when Luca finds out she's missing, he will lose his shit," I concluded.

"He hasn't found you in the last 3 months, you're obviously good at laying low."

"Her family would be devastated."

"Then let her leave a letter." Grace shrugged.

"We will get caught."

Looking over her shoulder, "Aria is downstairs making breakfast, you won't get through without being seen." Pulling out a set of keys, she handed them to me. "Go down the staircase and keep left. There's the side door you can get out of clear from anyone seeing you. My car's there. I'll keep Aria distracted. Go."

"No one can know I was here."

"I know," she nodded. "Call it even."

Grace paid her dues tenfold. "You could have called it even a long time ago."

"You saved my life, there's nothing I could have done to make up for that. But now, I'm saving yours. So my debt is paid."

"What are you going to tell them?"

"Nothing."

Chapter Twelve

I watched Bethany's chest rise and lower as she slept under the covers. My eyes slowly traced the curves of her body while I held her tenderly. Even through layers of clothing and a thick comforter, I could still visualize her naked body. A body that was always receptive to my touch. Her blond hair cascaded onto the pillow and some errant strands fell on her face, framing her soft features. Looking at her smooth porcelain skin and rosy lips made my dick swell with desire against my briefs. Closing my eyes to settle down the urge to bury myself deep inside her, I grabbed my crotch as though commanding it to behave. Since we arrived at my place back in Reykjavik, I'd devoured her body and claimed her until she fell asleep from exhaustion.

The whole week, I watched her every move, and when I blinked, my heart ached for her. What hurt the most was the inflicted pain she caused herself. She was never one to cross that line and I was the reason she did. Flashes of Marie each time I closed my eyes made me get sick. The scene in my mind was so vivid that I could still smell the blood everywhere.

Bethany raised her arm to rub her heavy eyelids and squirmed in pain. Slightly she opened her eyes. Her face lit up in a weak smile when she saw me looking at her.

"Don't you get tired of looking at me?"

"Not yet," I joked.

Truth to be told, getting tired of Bethany didn't seem possible.

"What's on today's agenda?"

"I want to take you to the Golden Circle," I replied. "End the day at the Blue Lagoon."

I'd been showing Bethany the area and how beautiful the country of Iceland was with its Northern lights, geysers, waterfalls, and volcanoes. She loved their Viking heritage and was eager to learn Icelandic which wasn't going well, but I enjoyed watching the effort.

As we got out of the car, Bethany began to giggle.

"What's so funny?" I asked.

"It will always make me laugh how you went from those fancy sports cars to this," she pointed to my Toyota Land Cruiser.

"It's practical for this kind of terrain," I scoffed. By no means was I happy about it, but I didn't want to attract attention to myself, plus driving a sports car on these rugged roads would destroy it.

There was a pathway from the parking lot of gravel that led to the Blue Lagoon. The pathway was made of brick but to the right and left were piles of volcanic rocks. The gush of wind hitting my face felt nice as I was bundled up in a heavy jacket and scarf. Once inside and got our day pass, Bethany and I went our separate ways. I headed to the men's locker room while she went to the women's locker room. It was mandatory to undress and shower using their natural spring soap before entering the lagoon water.

As I waited at the entrance of the Lagoon, my eyes observed the surroundings. It was a habit I couldn't shake off but now more so since having Bethany with me. There were people of all ages coming in and out of the water. Jealously rose within me when I saw Bethany walk out in a skimpy two piece bathing suit. Her eyes were set on me, but I could see the men around checking her out. The black material clung to her body so tight it looked about ready to rip. Her self-inflicted wound healed very well. The only bruises on her skin were from my own marking.

As she walked over to me she raised her brow, "Don't get upset. Next time don't take me somewhere that requires minimal clothing."

I wrapped my arm around her waist and pulled her close to me. "You're asking for it."

She smirked, "Whenever, wherever, however you want." Placing her hand on my bare chest she glided it down to my navel and down to the hem of my trunks.

"I will hold you to that," I replied placing a kiss on her plum lips. We weren't in Chicago anymore – we didn't need to hide or be afraid to be caught.

The Blue Lagoon was a breathtaking sight as the sun began to set, casting a soft golden light over the surreal landscape. The air was crisp as we stepped into the warm, mineral rich water; the geothermal heat enveloped us like a comforting embrace, creating a perfect contrast to the cool air.

Steam rose gently into the air from the blue water, blurring the edges of the surrounding lava fields making it hard to see other people around us. The lagoon had piles of volcanic rock strategically placed creating different sections for people to explore. We entered a little cave that blocked the wind and held the steam which created a foggy area. We stood in the center face to face as the velvety feel of the water warmed our skin.

As we walked deeper into the lagoon, the milky blue water shimmered around us. The atmosphere was serene, with the only sounds being the gentle lapping of water and the occasional laughter of other visitors. I looked at Bethany, her face illuminated by the soft light, and felt a rush of warmth in my chest. We found a quiet corner of the lagoon, where the waters were a deeper blue, almost like a hidden oasis. Taking a moment to admire Bethany's beauty, her hair clung around her wet body, droplets of water glistening on her skin. Somehow, without words or touching, it felt as though our connection strengthened in this very moment.

I leaned closer, our foreheads nearly touching, and whispered, "What do you think?"

Bethany smiled, her eyes sparkling with joy. "It's like a dream," she replied, her voice barely above a whisper.

As if responding to the magic of the moment, she leaned in for a soft kiss, the warmth of the water surrounding us adding to the intimacy of the setting. Her cheeks were flushed as the warmth between us was electric – an undeniable magnetism. As the sun continued its descent, painting the sky with shades of pink and orange, I brushed a strand of her hair behind her ear.

My fingertips lingered against her skin. "You're beautiful." My intense gaze locked onto hers.

The world faded away as we both solely focused on one another. I cupped her face into my hands, my thumbs brushing against her cheekbones. Our breaths mingled as the moment stretched between them heavy with anticipation. Leaning into one another, our lips met with a soft kiss that quickly deepened into a more passionate one that had our tongues in an entanglement. My hands moved to her waist pulling her close while her fingers threaded through my hair. Time seemed to stand still as an unspoken shared dream to have this moment become a permanent reality danced around us. When we finally pulled away, both of us breathless and smiling, the last rays of sunlight cast a golden glow over her face. Leaning my forehead against hers, our hearts raced in unison.

"I could stay like this forever," Bethany whispered softly. "Please say it's possible."

It wasn't possible for me to promise such a thing, but I couldn't disappoint her either. This was a moment suspended in time, defined by love and the serene beauty of this woman before me.

"Anything can be possible."

A sincere smile crossed her face. "I've never been happier."

"You don't miss Chicago?" I asked.

She shrugged, "I'd much rather be here with you."

Rephrasing it, "You don't miss your family?"

"Just as much as you miss Cassie." Her emerald eyes sparkled through the mist of fog.

Seductively, Bethany swayed her hips in the water as she glided toward the open area outside the cave. Following behind her, I breathed in the thin crisp cold air. My eyes wandered from observing the area and Bethany. Six months out of the lifestyle yet I couldn't shake off all the years I spent being Consigliere. The constant people watching, looking over my shoulder, taking extra precautions.

We sat on a ledge in the water waiting for our masseuse to get us.

"What would make you the happiest right now?"

It was a random question. "I have all I want right here."

"How long do you think Luca will allow this?" Her voice dipped low.

Sensing it was a real concern, I held her hand and kissed the top of it. "Let's just enjoy the moment."

"I don't want it to end."

"We'll always have Iceland," I grabbed her chin and placed a kiss on her lips.

It seemed to have helped ease her mind for the time being.

"Should I pick a name as well? You go by Jim so I need a name too."

"What are you thinking?"

"Something Viking-ish."

I couldn't help but laugh. "You've thought about this already so just spit it out."

"Freya."

"Not bad."

"Mr. Albertsson are you and your guest ready for your massages?" An attendant approached us.

We were taken to a secluded area where there were two masseuses waiting by two floating mats and light background music. Instantly, I was regretting this but there was no going back now. Bethany wanted to try this in-water massage that one of the spa techs stated "unlocks higher levels of well-being for your mind, body, and spirit with the revitalizing powers of geothermal seawater."

I feel like an idiot floating on this mat draped in a warm blanket with cucumbers on my eyelids but my body felt relaxed for the first time in what felt like forever. There was a sudden change in music from a soft melody to a lyrical song. The more I listened to it, the more it sounded familiar. Honing in on the words, I realized it was in a different language. It's Sicilian. That's odd to be playing it here.

La mafia e li parrini (The Mafia and the priests)

Si déttiru la manu (Shook hands with each other)

Poviru cittadinu (Poor citizen)

Poviru paisanu (Poor villager)

When I realized what the words were, I ripped the cucumbers off my eyelids throwing them into the water and quickly got onto my feet startling everyone.

"Is everything okay?" My masseuse asked.

"What happened?" Bethany questioned.

I huff, "Nothing. Just fell asleep and woke up." Playing it off as best as possible. Was I just being paranoid? Laying back on the mat, I tried to relax again. The masseuse placed the cucumbers back onto my eyes but I threw them into the water. She didn't say a word when I gave her a look, just a tight smile.

Unu isa la cruci (One raises the cross)

L'autru punta e spara (The other points and shoots)

Unu minaccia 'nfernu (One threatens hell)

L'autru la lupara (The other the shotgun)

It was a Sicilian song sung by Rosa Balistrei and written by the poet Ignazio Buttitta. The song was to call out the connection between the mafia and many priests during that time. Why would they play that here? My heart pumped in my chest, my mind immediately went to Cassie. Was this just a coincidence or was someone playing mind games with me? I was all too familiar with the strategy of mind games to instill lingering fear within someone.

The air was thick with the smell of espresso and the distant sounds of clinking glasses. A flickering overhead light cast shadows on the dark wooden table where Marco in a sharp suit, leaned back in his chair, a cigar nestled between his fingers. Across from him, I sat anxiously.

"You want to be a player in this game, Emilio? You gotta learn how to play with minds, not just muscles."

Confused, I question what I did wrong, "I mean, I'm no mind reader."

Marco chuckles softly, the kind of laugh that carries both amusement and a hint of menace.

"It ain't about readin' minds. It's about plantin' seeds. You see, people are like gardens. You just gotta know what to plant and when to water it." Marco takes a slow puff from his cigar, contemplating his next words. "Let's say you want to send a message to Giovanni, the butcher. He thinks he runs this

neighborhood. You want him to know you're the one in charge, but you don't want to spill a drop of blood. You don't just go up to him and tell him right?"

He offered me a cigar, which I knew I couldn't decline even though I wasn't a fan of them. So I took it and lightly puffed on it.

He says, "You see, words are powerful, but actions? They speak louder than a thousand whispers. You let him see something."

Marco reached for the newspaper then slid it across the table. I picked it up and read the front page revealing an image of the local butcher shop, its glass door shattered, blood staining the sidewalk. This sent more than just a message to the butcher, it was a warning for anyone else who wanted to test Marco's father.

My eyes widen, the weight of the implication sinking in. "So, that was you."

"You don't break his legs, you break his confidence. You let him know that if he's not careful, he might end up like that door."

"What if he goes to the cops?"

Marco leans back, a glint of amusement in his eyes. "That's where the games get interesting. You make him doubt. You make him think he's being watched, that he's surrounded. You send a little bird to whisper in his ear—there are eyes everywhere."

"What if he calls your bluff?"

"Fear is a tool, Emilio. Use it wisely. But remember, you can't just threaten; you have to charm as well. Make him think you're the friend he never knew he needed. Get him to trust you while you're tightening the noose."

I nod, absorbing the lesson, but a flicker of doubt crosses my mind. "What if it backfires? What if he doesn't care?"

Marco leans forward, his demeanor shifting from mentor to predator. "Then you remind him who he's dealin' with. You show him just how deep the roots of this garden run. Never forget, Emilio—every king has his pawns, but it's the king who controls the board."

He extinguished his cigar with a finality that echoed through the room.

"Rachel tells me you're street smart and I trust her judgment. I also don't forget those who helped my family. My wife is grateful that you saved her sister that night."

"I would only hope if one of my sisters were in that position someone would do the right thing too."

Marco taught me a lot of things and I'd only grown to perfect the art of mental warfare. Finding out who the target's closest friends were. Got to know their weaknesses. Then planted seeds and watched how they grew. I'd made a name for myself from it, so I knew the signs of them and I guaranteed it was being done now to me.

Chapter Thirteen

I did my best to enjoy the spa even though my skin crawled with paranoia. My gut said everything was fine but my mind was spiraling into madness. Bethany didn't seem to notice which made it easier to conceal my concern. The car ride home was long and by the time we got back we were starving.

"Why don't we do dinner tonight at that place you keep eyeing?" I suggested.

"Sjávargrillið? That'd be nice. Not sure I have anything nice enough to wear."

"Maybe you need to look a little harder."

Scratching her head, she sat up in the bed. Getting out of bed, I walked over to the closet and pulled out a dress she had been eyeing at a local boutique. It was an olive green long sleeve form fitting dress that hit her mid thigh. As I pulled it out, I held it out for her to see.

A big smile crossed her face, "Emilio, you didn't have to buy me anything."

"I figured you'd feel more like yourself if you were dressed up for dinner."

Jumping to her feet she gave me a big hug. "I'll go shower."

When the room was cleared, I grabbed my phone. In order for me to have peace of mind, I needed to make sure my communication through Father Joel wasn't exposed. For years I was in the know of everything. I knew what was going on at every given moment. Since being gone, the stress of it fell off my shoulders but now I felt the burden of it on my chest heavier than ever.

I walked out to the balcony where the cool evening breeze gently caressed my skin and whipped out the phone from my pocket. The conversation started as usual.

"Bless me Father for I have sinned."

"There's no sin too great for the Lord to forgive my child," the familiar voice responded.

Father Joel was assuring me our communications were still private and safe.

"I'm feeling lost and confused."

"You must trust God has a plan and will reveal it in his own time. Job was a wealthy man who lost everything, including his children, to the devil. Job remained faithful to God and in the end, God rewarded Job's patience with twice as much as he had before."

Father Joel was letting me know that Nicoletta no longer had concerns about her daughter. Perhaps Bethany's note gave her a sense of ease? Were they not looking for her?

"God will always take care of his own," I said at last.

"Yes my child. Remain steadfast in prayers and let me know when the man above speaks to you."

"Thank you Father," I replied before ending the call.

"Who is that?" Bethany said from behind me.

Turning around to face her, I shot a smile in her direction. "Making reservations."

The restaurant had dim lighting and was very intimate. Chef Gunnar Gíslasonwas hosting and delivered an exquisite 5 course menu.

Wrapping the fork around her fingers she slowly stuck it into the skúffukaka rested on the fancy plate and then placed a piece into her mouth. The same mouth I used to shove my dick down that precious throat.

Her fingers traced along the neckline of her dress. My eyes drifted down to her chest, the scoop neckline allowed her breasts to be perfectly displayed. The more I looked at her somehow I fell more in love. She submitted to me in ways I didn't demand. Feeling her foot glide up my leg, she wanted me to take her right here in front of everyone. I enjoyed entertaining her little kinks but I had something else in mind tonight.

"Would the lovebirds like anything else for this evening?" The waiter said interrupting our moment.

"That will be all," I replied still gazing at Bethany, "Ready to get out of here?"

The sparkle in her eyes lit up with excitement. "I'm going to use the restroom first."

I watched her sway her hips as she walked away lost in what I was looking forward to doing to her.

"You always preferred kleina."

"What are you doing here Athena?" I spat out.

Athena didn't seem too happy with my coldness. "Dinner with my husband." She tilted her head to the side, "Your new play thing is really pretty although she seems a bit young."

My leg twitched under the table as I clenched my jaw. "Tell your husband I said hi."

"Do you know how I have to play stupid about not knowing where his passport is?" Her tone was irate.

"Should I hand it to him right now?"

With a smirk she shot back, "I always loved your adventurous side. Does your new toy enjoy the way I taste?"

This only irritated me more. "This isn't a game."

"Then stop playing with me." Athena wasn't looking to make this easy at all.

Looking in the direction of the bathroom, I saw Bethany walking back to the table.

"I'll hand it off tomorrow. Corner of Fischersund at 8am."

"I'll see you then," Athena winked but she lingered just long enough for Bethany to roach the table. Turning toward her she made a comment, "I have the same dress."

Bethany had a blank expression and smiled politely, "You have good taste then."

"So do you. Enjoy your night."

Bethany and I both watched Athena walk away.

"Who was that?" Bethany asked turning her focus back onto me.

"Wanted to know what dessert this was," I pointed to the skúffukaka. "Let's head out."

As I held Bethany close to me, I spotted Athena at a table with a man seated across from her. Athena must have sensed someone looking in her direction because we made eye contact. A sly smirk crossed her face – shit. I knew asking her for a favor was going to backfire. If I learned anything in this life – there was nothing like a scorned woman.

Chapter Fourteen

As I walked out of the bathroom, I saw Bethany standing on the balcony waiting for me just as I told her to. When that crisp air entered my lungs, I felt recharged. The sight of Bethany as she stood there with lustful eyes was something I'd never get tired of. Green rays of lights blasted across the night sky. The shade of the Northern lights matched Bethany's eyes. It felt like I was dreaming.

"Are you cold?" I asked as I stood in front of her.

"Hopefully not for long," Bethany smirked.

Her nipples poked through the fabric of her dress and I noticed they were missing something. Sliding the dress off her shoulder to expose her breast, I saw it was bare. When I removed the other strap, the same on the other. A gust of wind caused her to sharply inhale and arc her back causing her chest to rise up and out toward me.

"Why are these bare?" I ask as each thumb rubbed a nipple.

"You said to put on the clamps, you didn't specify where." Her eyes dart downward.

I thought my dick was going to explode through my pants. I'd pushed Bethany's limits sexually thinking each time I'd gone too far but she never complained. Pulling the fabric of her dress making it fall to the floor, I licked my bottom lip at the sight of her naked body. Her large breasts on display, nipples hard just how I liked them.

"Turn around," I demanded. "Hands on the railing."

Bethany did as she was told, and her body slightly bent forward while gripping the railing causing her ass to poke out perfectly. Pulling my hand back, I forcefully slam it onto her ass cheek causing an echo. Bethany let out a pant. Spanked again. And again. And again. Watching her flesh go from pink to pinker than red had me salivating at the mouth with desire. I didn't stop until an imprint of my hand was there.

There was something about this kind of skin-to-skin contact, so raw it created this amazing connection to Bethany. As my hand made contact with her bare ass dissipating from the point of contact throughout the rest of my body created this intense energy that ran through my body.

Stepping back, I enjoyed the view. Mine. All mine.

"Turn around."

Stepping closer to her again, I got down on one knee. The metal glistened between her lips as her juices coated the clamp. I knew she'd be sensitive to the touch and I wanted to take my time with her tonight. I was fighting the urge to fuck my name out of her mouth until her brain went numb. Dragging my pointer finger up her inner thigh, the metal glistened more and I could smell her arousal. Bethany gripped the railing in front of her.

My finger circled the outside of her lips and she began to tremble. Parting them with my thumb, her enlarged clit was begging to be set free of the clamp and touched. Removing the clamp, Bethany let out a deep breath. Parting her legs so that her pussy was on full display, I let the cold air hit it, watching Bethany try not to get unraveled so easily put a smirk on my face. I placed my mouth close to the throbbing clit and blew on it slightly making her body tense. Placing a kiss on it, I looked up to see Bethany looking at me already a mess.

"Not yet baby," I reminded her.

Wrapping my tongue about her clit, I pulled it into my mouth to suck on.

"Shit," Bethany panted.

One suck, two suck, three suck, bite ... she was soaked. As I trailed kisses up her body, I had both hands on her body gliding up with me as I got to my feet. Pushing both her breasts together, I inserted both nipples in my mouth. One suck, two suck, three suck ... bite.

Bethany let out a moan. My hands remained gripping her breasts as I continued my trail of kisses up to her neck.

"Undue my pants," I whispered in her ear as I slapped her bare ass.

Eagerly she began to unbuckle my belt.

"Slow," I demanded.

Her eyes pled to reconsider but she knew I wouldn't. As a reward, I slid one hand down to her clit and began to massage it. This made her content. When she finally got my pants undone, I pulled away from her. Watching her miss me, only from taking a step back, made me love her more.

When I stood in front of her again, I took her hand and put my dick in it. Bethany wasted no time wrapping her hands around my cock and gliding it up and down using her own juices as lubricant. I pulled her in and began to deeply kiss her. The taste of her wine still on her tongue. Reaching for her hands, I pulled them off the railing and wrapped her arms around my torso.

"When I get you into position, you have fun and don't hold back," I said against her lips. "Get comfortable."

With a simple nod, she placed her hands on my back. This wasn't going to be easy doing it in this position but the sight of her under this beautiful night sky, I couldn't resist. Interestingly enough it was Athena who introduced me to this. I didn't lack in the department of making a woman orgasm, but this specific technique prioritized the female pleasure more than I would have thought. It does jack shit for me as I preferred deep penetration, but I'd give up all my selfish pleasures to see Bethany drown in hers.

One of my hands made its way to her thigh, lifting it and letting her wrap her leg around my own thigh. I pulled her even closer to me so that her complete weight was on me. Guiding my erection, I placed the tip just at her opening while my rock hard shaft lay against her vulva. Bethany inhaled sharply as her body expelled more liquid. As it lay getting drenched in her juice, I felt light-headed. How badly did I want to plunge deep inside of her but this would be far better to experience.

My hands grabbed her ass tightly as I slowly rocked her hips upward and down until she found her rhythm. A light moan escaped her lips. Reminding myself not to take control, I buried my face into her neck to suck and nibble on. Her breathing picked up and I felt her nails dig into my skin. Bethany was so wet it was dripping down my leg making my cock twitch. Her clit throbbing against my shaft was sending me over the edge.

The tip of my cock slightly entered inside of her while she continued to grind against me. This was purely for clitoral stimulation, which she was thoroughly enjoying, and if I managed not to cum all over her then I'd be impressed. Bethany began moaning, trying to catch her breath, her leg around me locked, her nails dug into my back as she rocked against me harder and faster. My hands remained on her ass clutching onto those cheeks for dear life.

"Fuck," I said against her skin.

"Emilio...," Bethany could barely sound coherent.

"I want you to cum over and over for me. I want to stand in a puddle of your cum."

The tip of my cock felt her cum pouring out of her and her body trembled from an orgasm. Before her body could settle, I began rocking my hips against her, grinding as slowly as possible.

"Em-"

"Don't stop," I demanded. "I want you to cum until you forget your own name."

And so she did. Again, and again, and again. Each time the orgasm was more intense, and I was damn near cumming without even fully being inside of her.

With the last effort Bethany had within her to even speak, she panted "I can't-... it's your turn."

Smirking at her thoughtfulness, I hoisted her up by her thighs so that both legs wrapped around my hips and slammed her down onto my cock. She was soaked and my dick slid right in without any friction. We both let out a sound of relief and I wasted no time thrusting my hips against her so violently her breasts were flying everywhere. She lashed onto my shoulder and bit down hard while I rode out the violent pulsations firing off all over my body. Cum shot out of my dick so hard that I wouldn't be surprised if it came bursting out of her mouth. The feeling of hot liquid filling her, warming her and completing me – my face buried into her neck and hers into mine as our bodies seemed to sync as one.

My knees gave out and I fell to the floor with Bethany still wrapped around me. We remained still as I tried to catch my breath with my head resting on her shoulder.

Eventually, I looked up at her, taking in her messy hair and dewy eyes, "You're the ruin of me."

Feeling her body trembling, I got on my feet still holding onto her and brought her into the warm apartment placing us both on the sofa where we lay cuddled. I pulled her onto me so that her head rested on my chest as we lay there letting our bodies sync together. Her heart beat in perfect time with mine. Her hand found mine and our fingers intertwine speaking words unspoken. Synced to one another, my heart exploded. I'd never be the same man again and I didn't want to be if it meant having a life with her. Lifting her hand held in mine up to eye level I kissed it.

"Marry me," I said in a low calm voice not disrupting our position.

Bethany lifted her head to look at me in surprise. "What?"

"Marry me," I repeated. "Bethany DeCarlo, I want you to marry me."

Her eyes sparkled and a wide smile crossed her face as she collided her mouth with mine.

"Is that a yes?" I asked.

"Well I'm already married ... but Freya isn't."

"Fair enough. Freya, will you marry me?"

"Yes, ástin mín."

"What does that mean?" I'd been here longer than she had and I didn't know a lick of the language, mainly because I didn't care to learn.

"Ástin mín means my love."

My heart felt like it had grown two sizes. "I don't have a ring."

"A ring isn't important to me. I just want you." She rested her head back on my chest.

"I have an errand to run in the morning. We can go to a chapel afterward."

"Okay."

What I should have done is tell her what that errand is. If I was going to marry her, I should tell her the truth about everything. Wasn't that the right thing to do? I should start with easier things, like Athena. Before I could mention a thing, I heard Bethany snoring.

Chapter Fifteen

Bethany POV

I was not one that knew her way around the kitchen but here I was trying to make pancakes. Flour coated the kitchen countertop while I searched for the next ingredient. Did they not have pancake mix here? Dumping whatever I had into the trash, I grabbed my coat and scarf to walk down the street.

The crisp, chilly air filled my lungs as I stepped outside, and I could see my breath as it created a cloud around me. Mornings in Chicago were nothing like walking the streets of Reykjavik at this hour. The cold air invigorated my senses, making me feel alive and alert. The silence of the early morning was peaceful with only a few other early risers or locals on their way to work. The sound from the crunch of frost against the bottom of my shoe as I walked on the concrete sidewalk echoed down the block. The beauty and the charm of the city created a feeling of tranquility and wonder, making each day feel like a blessing. It was magical and I soaked up every second of it. There was something about being in a different country where we could live our lives freely without disturbance or the burden of living up to certain expectations.

The colorful houses, with their corrugated metal roofs and vibrant façades, popped against the backdrop of the clear blue sky. The sun had been rising earlier the last few days. A gentle breeze hit my face that carried the salty scent of the nearby ocean, mingling with the fresh air. The sounds of the city waking up—birds chirping, the distant hum of traffic, and the occasional laughter of children heading to school—filled the air. Unlike Chicago, where every turn was a building, my scene now was the stunning views of the surrounding mountains and the ocean. I was unsure how long I would be here for but this would forever be a memorable experience.

The aroma of freshly brewed coffee wafted out from nearby cafes, beckoning me to indulge but my heart was set on one particular bakery. As I approached the brightly decorated building, I entered and inhaled the sweet smells of pastry goodness. Back home I rarely indulged, but I could eat everything here in one sitting.

The person in front of me asked the girl over the counter, "What's fresh?" I could tell they were from out of town given they didn't have an Icelandic accent.

The girl smiled, "We just got a fresh batch of vanilla buns out of the oven."

"That sounds delicious. I'll take one of those. Anything I should try? It's my first time in Iceland."

"If you want to be really Icelandic, a blueberry and licorice bun."

I laughed to myself watching the person scrunch their face.

"Hjónabandssælais really good," I suggested attempting my best to say it correctly. "It's basically oats filled with jam. Or Pönnukökur." I pointed to it for reference after butchering the name. "It's almost like a crepe."

"Thank you," the person smiled, "I'll take what she suggested."

"Ah! I thought it was Sunday for a moment," the owner came out of the back with a smile as he placed a fresh tray on the rack.

"It's a special day today," I smiled from ear to ear.

"I created a new coffee flavor to try. It's a twist on ávaxtafrappó but hot! You must try it. Go have a seat and I'll bring it to you with the rest of your order."

"Thank you," I laughed unsure exactly what that meant. Ávaxtafrappó is a fruit Frappuccinoif I wasn't mistaken.

It was nice having people treat you with kindness when they didn't know who you were. It was always hard to tell when someone was being genuine. The café hummed with the soft chatter of early morning patrons, the air thick with the rich aroma of fresh pastries. Sunlight streamed through the large windows, casting a warm glow on the wooden tables and illuminating the faces of those gathered. I sat at a small table in the corner waiting for my coffee.

"Enjoy!"

The girl startled me. I may not be in immediate danger but I found myself constantly looking over my shoulder.

"I'm so sorry! Are you okay?"

I forgot I go by Freya now. Something I still needed to get used to. "I was just lost in thought. Thank you."

Taking a sip, the perfectly temperate coffee coated my mouth filling it with flavors of berries which only got better as it went down my throat. Looking at my watch, I knew I had some time to spare. Emilio said he would be gone for about an hour. My fingers absentmindedly tracing the rim of the coffee cup and watching the steam rise as my mind drifted to my family back home. As much as I was enjoying this bit of freedom, I missed everyone terribly – even Luca. My mind began to wonder if I missed my brother because Emilio was still alive. Did my relationship with Luca really depend on Emilio's life? Would anything have changed between us if I knew Emilio was still alive?

The sound of the door chiming caught my attention causing me to look up and watch a woman walk in, cheeks flushed from the cold outside. We make eye contact and she nodded her head to me. Did I know her or was I just being paranoid? Everyone here was so nice it made me feel out of touch with reality. Out of politeness, I nodded in return. Unable to take my eyes off of her, she looked like a Viking goddess. Her long hair braided and left over her shoulder to cascade down to her hip. Wearing a brown leather trench coat with sheep fur lining and boots, she was clearly a local.

After placing an order at the counter, she made her way toward me.

"Mind if I sit?" She asked me.

Without giving an answer, the woman plopped herself onto the chair. She didn't even bother removing her jacket.

"Do I know you?" I asked.

"No," she smiled. "I've noticed you frequent this bakery. Are you on holiday?"

"Just moved here," I smiled. "I'm Freya"

I watched her extend her arm to shake my hand while carrying a sly smile, "I'm Athena."

Chapter Sixteen

Athena's sly smile gave me an odd feeling.

"I've seen you before." It was coming back to me. Her familiar face from last night that looked different when her hair was down. "Last night at Sjávargrillið. You've been watching me and not just because you're looking for friendly conversation."

"We have a lot more in common than the same dress in our closet."

I felt my face burning up. "Is there something you need to tell me or are you a bitter ex?"

She was stunned by my forward remark. The barista brought her drink, and she wrapped her hands around the warm cup, seeking comfort in its heat.

"I think you know we both have had that handsome man, 6'3, dark hair, with a five o'clock shadow that perfectly shades his jawline draped over our bodies."

Was she ... fantasizing about Emilio out loud or describing him that way to me to get under my skin? I shouldn't be surprised that Emilio took a lover but it still bruised my ego. This was what he felt every time he saw me with Pio.

"The difference between us, Athena, is you're living in your memories while it's my reality. Jim should have told you about me."

"So, you and Jim are together," Athena began, taking a sip of her coffee, her gaze steady on me. "That's... interesting."

"Is it?"

"One second he's out of town, next thing you know he's back here, with you." Her eyes flashed a hint of sadness.

"I'm sorry if he didn't give you proper closure. But it's better to put the past behind you."

"It's not that far behind," Athena leaned in, "You may be lying in his bed now but I've been in there enough to have the mattress stained with my cum from painting my body with his tongue."

A vile feeling took over as I did my best not to lash out at her. "Now that I'm back in the picture, you're no longer needed."

"I don't mind sharing you know."

"Well I do."

"You're going to have to get over that." Athena's nose flared and her brow furrowed. "After all he does have two hands, one fist to stuff each of us."

An eruption of vomit hit my throat and I swallowed it quickly, taking the burn of the acid. I had no intentions of sharing Emilio, but it seemed they had been doing things within a short time that I hadn't even done with him the last few years.

"Two is company – three's a crowd." Was the only thing I could muster up trying to hold back tears.

Athena glared at me. "You may have had him first but I still linger in the back of his mind."

"Very confident of yourself."

"He seemed to enjoy experiencing filling all three holes at once – claimed he'd never done such a thing. It was a first for us both."

It was a slap in the face but I wasn't going to show her she succeeded in getting under my skin. I'd had enough of this and got to my feet graciously.

Bending down to her ear, I sternly voiced, "Understand one thing here. I was already breathing the air around him before you came along. And since he hasn't made it clear – let me do the honor – he's mine. You were just a play thing to distract him until we were able to be together again. I could have felt sorry for you... instead I pity you."

With that, I walked out and never looked back. I wanted this chance to become someone new, someone different than Bethany. Freya was going to be different. A chance at being reborn and a new persona – I should take full advantage of it. Carrying my box of pastries in hand, I walked with a strong stride back to the apartment.

By the time I reached the door, my mind was clear and free from that woman and wanted to waste no time setting up a lovely breakfast for me and my soon to be husband. Stepping inside the small apartment, I was hoping to see Emilio back but figured it'd be better if he came home to something more than just breakfast. Quickly putting the pastries into a plate and setting the table for two, I ran into the bedroom and pulled out a piece of lingerie I bought the other day.

Just as I finished connecting the straps, I heard the key lock on the door being turned so I ran out toward the kitchen and quickly hopped onto the table with a cream puff placed between my legs. My exposed nipples hardened at the thought of being touched. Thinking on the spot, I grabbed one of the napkins and wrapped it around my mouth securely tying it behind my head. Emilio had tied me up plenty of times, blindfolded me, even the occasional cutting of airflow but clearly his tastes had changed. I refused to let that woman satisfy his needs – if his desires had become more demanding then I would fulfill them.

My body stiffened hearing the key turning in the lock and the door opening. I wasn't sure what to expect but I was diving all in. When Emilio came into sight, he seemed irritated but when he saw my little setup his mood shifted. The facial expression on Emilio's face was one that my heart picked up its pace. That smoldering look, the lust in his darkened eyes, and the sense of need consumed me.

"This is new," he commented as he walked toward me.

"You like it?" I giggled as there wasn't much to the outfit. It had a thin strap over my breast and a thinner strap barely covering my lower region.

"Sorry I took so long," he took some whipped cream off a pastry with his finger and smeared it across my lip.

"I'm sure you'll make it up to me." Sticking my tongue out, I licked my lip and then took his finger into my mouth slowly pulling it out. "Figured we'd do something ... different."

"What do you have in mind?" The sparkle in his eyes made me wonder how far he would actually go with me.

"I want you to do to me anything you want."

"You let me do that every time." He held my chin with his pointer.

"You're holding back. I know you are. So I want you to let loose."

Emilio slightly tilted his head to the side. "What makes you think I'm holding back?"

I shifted my weight onto my knees. "I want you to fill every hole. At once."

Pausing for a moment, Emilio then stepped back giving me a questioning look until it sunk in where I got the idea from. It pained me to know Athena flashed into his mind at this very moment.

"No." Emilio seemed to be angry.

"Why not?" I asked getting off the table. As I walked toward him, I let it out, "Athena seemed to enjoy it. Why can't I?"

"What else did she say?" Emilio scoffed.

"Enough to know you've developed a new taste. And I want in on it."

"I don't think you're able to handle it."

"Let me decide that."

Emilio's chest rose as he inhaled deeply and then slowly let out a breath of air. Debating whether to proceed, he eventually gave in.

"There's no going back," he warned.

"Good."

A smoldering look crossed his face again making me melt on the inside. I watch as he opened a cabinet and pulled out a jar of liquid. Confused, I walked over to him to see what it was. Coconut oil.

"You never have issues getting me wet," I commented.

"I'll need this to achieve my goal," he replied opening the lid.

Placing the jar on the little island in the kitchen, Emilio hoisted me up seating me beside the jar. The cold countertop hardened my nipples. He undid the skimpy outfit I had on so that I was naked and pulled the hair tie out of my hair so that it fell down my back. Taking the jar, he began to lightly pour the oil onto my shoulder and across my chest. The silky texture of the liquid dripped down my body as I waited for Emilio to touch me. As he began to massage my shoulders, the warmth of his hands melded with the oil, creating an intoxicating sensation. Applying gentle pressure, his thumbs dug into my shoulders allowing my body to relax. His fingers working their magic, gliding over my skin, tracing the contours of my collarbone, making their way to my breasts.

Catching his gaze the intensity in his eyes ignited a spark. It never got old. There was something electric about the way he touched me, no matter what kind of pressure, there was always a mix of tenderness and desire that made my heart race. Taking a breast in each hand, he massaged them tenderly, the oil creating a glistening trail down my body that seemed to shimmer in the morning light. His thumbs circled my nipples as he continued to massage my breasts, each swirl deliberate and slow as he took in every curve. I felt his touch deep within me causing a rush of warmth that spread through me like fire.

The air was thick with the blend from the sweet scent of the coconut oil mingling with the faint sound of distant waves crashing against the shore outside the window. The intimacy of the moment enveloped us like a soft blanket.

"You're beautiful," he commented as his hands slid down right under my breast gripping my waist, causing me to arch my back, pushing my nipples further into his direction. His thumbs sunk into my ribs and his fingers into my back as my chest and stomach were coated in oil. The act was simple but so erotic that a moan broke from my mouth – the sound spurred him on. "Not yet my love, you're in for a ride."

He pulled my body toward him so forcefully that our mouths collided, my legs wrapped around his hips and my arms wrapped around his neck. My breasts squished against his hard chest as my every curve melted into every muscle of his which ramped up my need to have him inside me. Needing skin to skin, I pulled up his shirt, we only broke contact when he pulled the shirt over his head, then we were back at it. Emilio's lips attacking mine with force, his mouth keenly exploring mine as he grabbed a fistful of my hair.

His free hand made its way up my inner thigh and to my lips. Circling around them before sliding one finger rubbing my clit for a moment before lowering to my opening. Releasing his hand gripping my hair, he unwraps my legs from his body. Placing the heels of my feet at the edge of the counter, my legs are spread open for him. Sliding a second finger inside me, he hooked them as they entered and exited my body.

"Ready for another?" He breathed.

Nodding, I braced myself. He removed his fingers and dunked his hand into the jar of coconut oil taking a handful before entering back inside of me. Using the oil as lube, all three fingers slide inside me with a bit more ease. While thrusting his fingers in and out of me, his thumb made its way to my clit slowly stimulating it. My breath picked up as my body was enjoying the sensation I was already getting. A moan escaped my mouth.

"Can you take more?"

"Yes, more," I panted.

In slid another finger and I fell back onto my hands placed behind me with my head dropping back. My breasts were on full display and I felt his mouth close on my nipple. The sound of my juices with the oil mixed with my heavy breathing filled the air. The smell of coconut filled my nostrils.

"Emilio," his name came out like a song.

"Is this good for you?"

"Oh my god," I panted, "More. More."

With a smirk, Emilio entered a fourth finger, lightly jiggling his fingers inside me mimicking a vibrator. In and out, he made sure he pushed all four fingers inside me deeply as his tongue continued to wrap around my nipple, massaging it, causing me to continue moaning in pleasure.

"I'm going in," he said biting down on my nipple.

Between his bite and forcefully pushing his fist inside me, I gasped. It felt as though my body no longer needed air to survive. Falling onto my back, Emilio's mouth found its way to my clit simultaneously as he continued to twist his fist inside of me. I was beginning to see stars as he began gently thrusting his fist inside of me. It was such an intense feeling that I would have never expected to enjoy. But this was more than just sex – it was emotional. It felt like I was giving my body and soul to him fully – transitioning into a spiritual experience uniting us as one, transcending me to be bound to him for life.

Emilio's fist was thrusting harder, his mouth sucking on my clit with equal intensity. I grabbed the edge of the countertop with both my hands to hold myself in place. My body was in overdrive as I was crying out in pleasure so loudly, I felt the vibration through my body. Completely taken over by getting fist fucked, I hadn't noticed Emilio unzip his hands until I felt the pressure of his cock enter my rectum. He stood in front of me, his mouth soaking wet, but the wild look in his eyes told me he was enjoying this just as much as I was.

"All three," he panted in excitement.

He shoved his free hand into my mouth, his fingers rested on my tongue slightly hitting the back of my throat. I was undone. Every spot the vagina had was getting stimulated all at once. My body began to convulse. Multiple orgasms ruptured through my body making my eyes roll back as if I'd lost complete control of myself. I didn't feel Emilio pull his hand out of my mouth or his dick from my anus. My body was on a euphoric high that I didn't think I would come back from.

"I'm going to go slow," Emilio said as his fist thrusting slowed down while coming down from his own high. "Exhale and relax yourself so that I can pull out my hand."

I did as I was told and lay on the countertop completely satisfied. The smell of coconut was still in the air, and the sound of the waves in the distance still crashed against the shore – only this time the essence of love danced in the room.

Managing to sit up so that I was face to face with Emilio, he whispered into my ear, "It meant nothing with her. Every time I closed my eyes, I saw you. It was always you in my mind."

Chapter Seventeen

Emilio POV

The icy winds howled outside the cozy cabin, the sound echoing off the surrounding mountains like a warning. Inside, the warmth of the fireplace flickered against the walls, casting dancing shadows that mirrored the tumultuous feelings in my heart. I found this intimate place and called for an officiant to meet us here. Entering the room, I saw Bethany standing by the window, gazing at the ethereal beauty of the snow-capped peaks and the shimmering Northern Lights that painted the night sky in hues of green and violet. This was a place of magic, a sanctuary far removed from the constraints of her life back home.

Her presence always ignited a spark of warmth within me. I could never understand how she had that much power over my heart. I moved closer, wrapping my arms around her waist, resting my chin on her shoulder.

"It's beautiful, isn't it?" I murmured, my breath tickling her ear.

"It is," she replied softly, though her voice betrayed the turmoil brewing inside her. "Feels surreal – being here with you ready to take our vows."

Sensing Bethany wished her family could be here, that they could be so accepting of this, made me question if this was the right thing to do. As much as I wanted to marry Bethany, casting her feelings away like how she'd been treated her whole life seemed selfish of me to let her go through with this.

I turned her gently to face me, my dark eyes searching within hers for the truth behind her hesitation. "We don't have to go through with this."

Bethany POV

"I just wish Luca would have just accepted you and me together," I whispered, my heart racing at the thought of defying my brother without him interfering or facing repercussions. I could barely look Emilio in the face.

I sighed, feeling the weight of guilt pressing down on me like the heavy snow that blanketed the ground outside. Luca, always the protective guardian, had made it clear that he disapproved of Emilio. "He's not good enough for you," he had said, his tone filled with authority. But I knew better; it wasn't that Emilio wasn't good enough for me, it was that I wasn't good enough for Emilio.

Emilio cupped my face in his hands, his touch tender yet firm. "Our love means everything to me Bethany. If that means not going through with this for the sake of your sanity then so be it. I'd rather you be happy than regret marrying me. It's just a piece of paper."

His words struck a chord within me, resonating with the quiet longing I had carried in my heart. "I've never wanted anything more than to be your wife. I'd give up everything for this to be forever," I admitted, my voice barely a whisper. "I just can't help thinking how I destroyed your life and after everything Luca has done for me – I took away the one person he relied on. You were more like a brother to him than I am a sister."

"You didn't destroy my life, I did that on my own." Looking into my eyes with such determination in his gaze and the unwavering belief he had in our love, he confessed something I needed to so desperately hear, "But I don't regret it. If it led us here. I won't regret it."

I let out a breath with a newfound strength surging within me. "Ástin mín, let's get married."

The smile on Emilio's face gave me reassurance that we would live a happy life.

"Follow me," he said taking my hand.

"Where are we going?"

"Let me at least do one thing."

Grabbing our coats, we made our way out of the room. Opening the door to head outside, I wasn't sure what to expect. The moon hung low in the sky, illuminating the landscape with a silvery glow, making the snow sparkle like diamonds. As we arrived at the clearing, Emilio stood behind me as we looked up into the night sky. The Northern Lights danced overhead, casting a surreal light that made the world around us feel ethereal. Emilio turned me around to face him, pulling me closer as our breaths mingled in the frigid air.

I watched as he got down on one knee and spoke such loving words, "Bethany DeCarlo. The light of my life, the center of my world, the woman I will die loving. Will you marry me?" His voice low and full of reverence.

Emilio reached into his pocket, pulling out a small, delicate ring with a pear-shaped diamond, the band glinting in the moonlight. "It's not what you deserve. It was a last minute purchase, and once we are back in the city, I will get you a proper one."

"Yes," I answered. My heart swelled as he slipped the ring onto my finger, the simple yet beautiful design a symbol of our commitment. I didn't need the fancy material things or to be draped in diamonds, this was more than enough. "Emilio, it's beautiful," I breathed, tears welling in my eyes.

"Just like you," he replied softly, brushing a strand of hair behind my ear as he got to his feet.

I would have been satisfied getting married in this very moment, right now under the night stars. We kissed – the world fading around us.

Emilio POV

It wasn't the traditional wedding I ever thought it would be, but our love wasn't the traditional kind. As the sun began to rise over Kvernufoss, its golden rays illuminating the cascading waterfall, I stood at the edge of the misty clearing, my heart pounding with a mixture of excitement and anticipation. Deeply invested in the Icelandic heritage, Bethany planned our ceremony outdoors as she claimed it was to "connect us to the elements of earth, water, air and fire." I didn't give a shit what kind of ceremony she wanted as long as she was happy. The sound of rushing water filled the air, creating a symphony of nature that perfectly matched the fluttering in my chest. Dressed in a crisp, navy suit that contrasted beautifully with the lush greenery surrounding me, I adjusted my tie, the cool breeze sending shivers down my spine. The towering cliffs of moss-covered rock loomed above me, forming a breathtaking backdrop for the momentous occasion that lay ahead. I took a deep breath, inhaling the fresh, earthy scent of the landscape, and pictured Bethany standing before me, her smile radiant against the stunning natural beauty. Today, under the watchful gaze of the waterfall and the vast expanse of the sky, I would vow to love her for eternity, embracing the adventure that awaited us.

Bethany POV

As the first light of dawn broke over Kvernufoss, illuminating the majestic waterfall and casting a gentle glow on the lush greenery surrounding me, I stood nervously in the secluded glade, my heart racing with excitement. The cool mist from the cascading water kissed my skin, mingling with the delicate floral scent of the wildflowers that adorned the area. Dressed in a flowing, light pink gown that danced around my ankles, I adjusted the lace-trimmed veil that framed my face, glancing at my reflection in the mirror. Admiring having done my own hair, the front sections braided and pinned back as the rest of my hair flowed freely in waves under the veil. The sound of rushing water outside the cabin placed near the waterfall provided a soothing soundtrack as I took a moment to breathe deeply, allowing the beauty of the landscape to ground me amidst the whirlwind of emotions. I envisioned Emilio waiting just beyond the curtain of water, our love made tangible in this breathtaking setting. Today, in this enchanting haven, I would make a promise that would bind our hearts together forever, surrounded by nature's splendor and the magic of the moment.

A knock at my door by the girl at the front desk told me it was time. I chose Kvernufoss Mountain due to the seclusion yet serenity the location gave. It was perfect for our intimate celebration given it was only Emilio, myself, the priest, and our witness. As I made my way toward Emilio who was beside the priest, I couldn't help but smile from ear to ear. With the backdrop of the cascading waterfall, this moment couldn't have been more perfect.

Even though this was an elopement, I wanted this ceremony to be deeply tied to Iceland's cultural heritage. As we stood face to face, Emilio took my hands in his, our fingers tightly entwined in front of us while the priest began to speak.

"Jim, do you promise to love, to stand by, and to cherish Freya no matter what?" The priest voiced.

"I promise to love you, to stand by you, to cherish you, no matter what." Emilio was never emotional; this was the first time I heard him get choked up.

Tears streamed down my cheeks as I replied, "And I promise to love you fiercely, to support you, and to choose you every single day."

Underneath the vast, open sky, we exchanged our vows, pure and heartfelt, sealing our commitment in the sacred space of that moment.

"I pronounce you husband and wife. You may kiss the bride."

Emilio placed a soft kiss on my lips as his hands were placed on my hips. In this moment, it was just the two of us, bound by love and the promise of forever. We had chosen each other, against all odds, and nothing would ever change that. We snapped out of the moment just as we heard someone clapping their hands. As we both turned our heads, we saw a man, with half a slightly disfigured face, smirking in a sinister way.

"That was beautiful," his raspy voice buzzed through the air.

Emilio without looking at me stood in front of me. "Bethany, run."

Chapter Eighteen

I might not know the face but I sure as hell knew the sound of that voice. It was the same voice that held a gun to my head while handing over the duffle bag. I'd never forget that voice. How the hell did he find me? I made sure I was cautious leaving Chicago the same way I left the first time. After I had gotten my ticket, I knew I needed to swap my boarding pass. It was easy when I spotted a young college kid and convinced him now was the time to explore the world and traded tickets with him. Then, to be extra cautious, I swapped my ticket with a random person who was ordering coffee at one of the gates.

The man, who I recalled being called Birdy, stood with his arms across his chest and a smirk that I wanted to slap off his face. He was about my height but had a wide bulky frame. My first thought when I heard his voice was to tell Bethany to run but I should have known there would be others here to hone us in. The scream of Bethany behind me as someone grabbed her pulled at my heart.

"Let go of me!" Bethany screeched.

"What is going on here?!" The priest asked concerned and fearful.

Bang. Bang. I heard the gunshots and two bodies dropped behind me. Bethany screamed as she witnessed the priest and our witness get shot. Everything seemed to be moving in slow motion, and the cold air was starting to sink into my skin.

Birdy began walking toward me as the man holding Bethany came into view. He was very young, with a baby face and blond golden curly hair.

"You could have just called," I said to Birdy.

"You seemed to have left the phone at the airport along with the duffle bag. Didn't leave behind the money though," he scoffed.

That was another swap I did. After buying a new piece of luggage, I tossed the duffle bag and stuffed the new luggage with the cash.

"You were stupid to go back to Chicago. Did you really think we wouldn't keep an eye out for you to return?"

"If you have been following us the last 2 weeks, then why wait to show your face now?" I asked.

"Watching the sheer panic on you is more fun," Birdy said with a chuckle. "You should have seen yourself at the spa."

So I wasn't being paranoid, he was there watching. It sent a shiver up my spine. How did I let my guard down so easily?

"If you're here for me, I'll come willingly. Let the girl go." I shot back as though I was engaging in conversation when all I wanted to do was rip his head off.

"Emilio!" Bethany managed to wiggle free, but the young man grabbed her once again.

"It's okay," I assured her.

Birdy nodded to the young man to take Bethany away. She was resistant at first, but when I shot her a look to comply, she knew I couldn't get us out of this one. I watched as the young man took her to a nearby van, placed her inside, and drove off.

"We will keep her until we know you will fully cooperate. No funny business this time."

"Who is we?" I asked.

A sinister smile crossed his face. "You've been hunting us down for a while now."

The wheels in my brain were turning. The man at the spa, who left burned marks on Aria, he wasn't working alone. He had a team. The blood began pumping through my veins, I could feel it flowing against my skin.

"What do you want?"

Birdy pulled out a cigarette and offered me one from the pack. "Do as we say and she lives."

"I don't smoke," I replied. Since Bethany was with me, I hadn't smoked a single day since she came to Iceland.

"You can take the man out of the game, but you can't take the game out of the man." Birdy lit up the cigarette in his mouth and let out a puff. "It's only a matter of time before you dive back in. Might as well pick the stronger team."

"Stronger team?" I cleared my throat to hide from laughing in his face. "If you think lurking in the shadow makes you a strong team, you're all cowards – won't even show your faces."

Birdy pointed to the side of his face that was slightly burnt, "Do I look like a coward to you?"

I knew straight away he had no fears. There was a scar across his face and part of it looked burned. A million thoughts ran through my mind. Who, what, where, and why.

He went on, "Someone like me would get noticed easily amongst a crowd of people, but the one you should be afraid of most – the mastermind - has been lurking around you for years. Close enough to slit your throat."

My blood started to boil. If this was true then that means there was a rat. We don't take lightly to those. For it to happen under my watch meant it was someone I trusted.

"What do you want from me?"

"Come work for us."

"I don't know who us is."

"MC. He wants you on the team."

"MC?" I questioned hoping to get more information.

"Yeah. MC."

"Why?"

"You're good at what you do. Or do you not care for the girl? Banging your boss's sister is ballsy of you. Maybe we should go for Cassie."

The mention of my sister almost blinded me with rage. If I had a gun I'd shoot him in the face right now. "If you think I believe for a second that you know where my sister is, you are as dumb as you look."

See, Father Joel didn't even know where Cassie was hiding. Even if she was followed out of the Church, Cassie was good at losing someone on her tail. I made sure her place had a private escape. Our spot, a place neither one of us spoke about to anyone else, was truly a safe place. I was calling his bluff.

"I can call goldilocks and tell him to slit Bethany's throat."

There was nothing more I disliked than not having the upper hand.

"Why does this MC want me?'

"Wasn't an idea I was fond of. But you have the muscle and the knowledge needed for our plan to succeed."

"What exactly is the plan?" I questioned although I was certain it ended with death.

"MC will discuss that with you." Birdy held out the pack of cigarettes.

My hesitation was to make him wonder how serious I felt about Bethany. If I stalled then it showed no commitment; however, if I jumped on the opportunity to save her they would use her against me for anything.

I reached for the pack and pulled out a cigarette.

Chapter Nineteen

Bethany POV

"Now that's a sight," a man's voice echoed.

Frozen in place, I remained scrunched in a ball on a cold concrete floor with a blindfold on. I didn't remember how I got here. One minute I was pushed into a van and the next I woke up alone in a dark room with sunlight coming from a small tiny window at the top of the wall so out of reach.

Plenty of times Emilio coached me on what to do if I found myself in a situation while alone, but all of that left my brain the moment this man's cold voice hit my ears. I wouldn't even know how to get out of here.

"Being shy now?" He asked as his voice seemed to get closer.

Panic overwhelmed me as I felt his presence get closer. He knelt down close to my body.

"Don't worry, I don't plan on hurting you." His breath grazed my back giving me goosebumps. "Congratulations are in order. How does it feel having two husbands? Maybe we should fly to Spain and get hitched. I hear third times a charm."

"What do you want?" My body began trembling with fear.

"Your brother would be a good start. Are you willing to help me?"

"If you think I'd betray my brother, you might as well kill me right now."

Mockingly he laughed, "Not yet. Although, Emilio's cooperation will determine if you live. I'm a fair man. To make it equal, your cooperation will determine if he lives."

I could feel the sweat popping out of my pores, and my body began to shake in fear. "What makes you think I won't scream right at the top of my lungs?"

"What makes you think I won't cut out your tongue?" The man's words ran a chill through me. "Don't test me, I don't play nice."

My face became wet as tears poured out my eyelids and slid down against my skin. "There's nothing I can do to help you."

"Not true. I know you hold some valuable information I can use." His finger tangles into my hair as he pets me. "Tell me about Alfie."

If I wasn't visibly shaking before, I was now. "What about Alfie? He's just some kid my brother pulled off the streets."

"See ... I would believe that. Just one thing ... he looks a lot like his father."

Stay strong Bethany, don't break. "He doesn't even know who his father is, what makes you think I do?"

My head snapped back, he held a tight grip of my hair in his fist. "I got away with putting burn marks on Aria Cassariano, imagine what I will get away with doing to you with no one to come save you. They wouldn't even know where to look for your body."

He let go of me and I whimpered as I held my knees up to my chest. "My brother and his family were killed. I watched them be buried."

"I'm going to come back tomorrow," he tucked a strand of hair behind my ear. "If you have the same answer, I'm going to cut off that finger of yours with the ring and make you swallow it."

"Who are you?" I breathed as the vomit erupted up my esophagus but managed to hold it down.

"We know one another better than you think."

Terrified, I barely got the words out, "What?"

Placing his mouth beside my ear, he so politely stated, "I've been around you. Inside you. Watching you."

I felt the blood drain from my face. My mouth went dry, and I suddenly became nauseous. Inside of me? Suddenly a piece of cloth was shoved into my mouth almost making me choke on it. The man left and I was left alone. I spit out what was shoved in my mouth into my hand. I see they are a pair of panties. Examining them further, I realized they were mine by the initials BC in rhinestones. I was drawing a blank until it hit me causing me to crawl on my knees to an empty bucket and proceed to vomit. *I've been around you and inside you*. His words made me cringe. The man was the same person I engaged with for the first time at the sex party all those years ago with my old boyfriend. I never saw the man's face that night.

As though it wasn't enough that his voice disrupted my mind, and his touch crawled under my skin, the thought of how I used to fantasize about his touch caused such a vile feeling within me. He was everywhere undetected, and now it made me question how long he had been watching us all.

Chapter Twenty

The dim light of the single overhead bulb flickered as I paced the small living room, the tension in the air palpable from the disgust of what I had just done. I was counting down the seconds until I could see, feel, and inhale Bethany again. I placed the burner phone in my back pocket as I waited for Birdy to tell me what to do next. I never contemplated my life choices as much as I had the last few months. One choice changed my life forever.

Working for Marco had its bonuses, aside from the cash I made, I learned how to get creative when trying to get around undetected. Those first few years taught me a lot about myself and my capabilities which was crucial to my survival getting out of Chicago.

In the bustling airport, travelers rushed past me, their faces a blur of anticipation. It dawned on me that these men who saved me would be able to track me simply by checking the name on the passport they gave me. I wasn't looking to return the favor of them saving my life. Stopping to lean against a column, I scanned the crowd passing by. My eyes landed on a lanky guy with tousled hair and oversized headphones as he scrolled through his phone while walking. I watched him head toward the restroom where I followed him in.

Leaving his luggage and backpack behind him as he took a piss at the urinal to which I purposely knocked into. "I'm sorry man," I say as I neatly place his items behind him while swapping our boarding passes.

The kid looks over his shoulder, "It's all good."

Quickly I dashed out and purchased a carry-on from one of the shops. Finding another restroom, I transferred the money from the duffle bag to the carry-on suitcase quickly while in one of the stalls. It would be risky keeping anything they gave me so I tossed the duffle bag and burner phone in case they had any tracking devices installed on them. Making sure no one would be able to trace back to me, I couldn't risk that I was seen by anyone. Once that kid knew his ticket was swapped, the only person he'd interacted with that might have been odd would be when I knocked into his things. So, for an extra layer of protection, I found another person I could swap tickets with. Walking over to one of the bars stationed at a nearby gate, I saw a woman eagerly trying to get the bartender's attention as a voice on the loudspeaker called last call for boarding the plane. By the look of anxiousness, I could tell it was her flight. Swiftly I stood beside her unnoticed. With her purse opened wide, I reached in and took her boarding pass, wallet, and passport then quickly walked away. I tossed her wallet and passport in the trash. If she couldn't identify herself and she had no boarding pass then there was no way of her interfering. Sprinting to the gate, it wasn't until I sat in the seat that I realized the destination.

Iceland.

It was flawless and I did the same when I had Bethany come back with me. Where was my error? How did they find us? I paced the room, my mind going over every detail.

Suddenly, I heard the unmistakable sound of footsteps pounding up the stairs outside my door.

Chapter Twenty-One

Immediately, I pulled out a hidden gun under the coffee table. The footsteps sounded urgent and there was no reason why Birdy needed to be in a rush. Slowly walking toward the door, I shut the light off so they would think no one was home. The door burst open, slamming against the wall with a force that rattled the frames.

A man stood in the doorway, his face flushed with rage, eyes wild like a storm. We made eye contact.

"You!" He shouted holding a sleek black pistol pointed directly at my chest, his hands trembling with a mix of fury and disbelief. "You're the one sleeping with my wife!"

Shit. Athena's husband. Holding my gun up pointing toward his head, dead in my tracks, "Calm the fuck down!"

His voice thundered, echoing off the walls. "You think you can just take her from me? You think I wouldn't find out?"

My heart raced, adrenaline coursed through my veins. He didn't look like he had the guts to kill someone. Tossing my gun on the sofa and raising my hands slowly, palms out. "Listen man—"

"Shut up!" He interrupted, stepping into the apartment, the gun unwavering in his grip. "You think you can just sleep with my wife and walk away like it's nothing? You're dead wrong."

The room felt small, even smaller than it was, the walls closing in as I tried to find the right words. "I didn't mean for it to happen —"

"Spare me the excuses!" He shouted, advancing. "You didn't just 'accidentally' sleep with her. We've been married 10 years!"

My mind raced, and I could feel the weight of this man's accusations pressing down on me. Athena was just meant to mend my broken heart and the thrill that had led us down this dark path meant nothing to me. But now, all that mattered was surviving this moment.

"No, I didn't," I confessed. "But it's over now. Why don't you put the gun down," my voice steady despite the chaos. "Let's talk this out. Violence isn't the answer."

"Talk?" He manically laughed - a harsh, bitter sound. "What's there to talk about? You've ruined my marriage!"

With a sudden motion, he lunged forward, swinging the gun toward me. In a split second, I dove to the side, narrowly avoiding the shot that rang out, shattering a lamp and sending shards of glass flying across the floor.

"Get back here!" He roared, his face twisted with rage.

Scrambling to my feet, adrenaline surged as I ducked behind various furniture while tossing things in his direction. The apartment felt like a war zone, each breath I took heavy with the scent of fear. I could hear the man moving around the room, searching for me.

"Come out, you coward!" He shouted, his voice echoing off the walls. "You think you can hide?"

I could take the easy way out right now, blast his head off, but I'm already on the run, and I don't have any connections here to save my ass. I scanned the room for anything I could use and spotted a heavy metal vase on the shelf and grabbed it, clenching it tightly in my hand.

The man's voice was a low growl and the frustration boiled beneath the surface. "You've taken everything from me!"

As I heard him getting closer, I bolted from behind the couch, swinging the vase with all my strength. It connected with the man's arm, causing him to stumble back, the gun momentarily slipping from his grip. Lunging for the weapon, we both hit the floor, wrestling for control of the closest gun. The man was strong, fueled by rage, but I fought back with desperation, managing to twist the gun from his hand and scrambling to my feet.

"Just think about Athena!" I shouted, keeping the gun pointed at him. "You don't want to ruin everything more than it already is!"

For a moment, he hesitated, anger flickering in his eyes as he processed my words. The tension hung thick in the air, both of us breathing heavily, caught in an unnecessary moment. Rage will overpower a man's logic, and he wasn't going to stop until he got a piece of me. Getting onto his feet, his expression narrowed, and he lunged again. I sidestepped, managing to dodge his direct hit, and the two of us collided against the wall. The gun slipped from my grip, clattering to the floor.

Chaos ensued as fists flew in a flurry of anger and frustration. He managed to land a hard punch to my jaw, sending me staggering back, but quickly I recovered, using the momentum to tackle the man onto the coffee table, which splintered beneath us.

My hand wrapped around his neck in an attempt to cut off his oxygen flow. "I'm not your enemy. I'm not the one who betrayed you."

The man's eyes widened and then his body slightly calmed down as he realized I was right. Helping him up to his feet, he gave me a nod. Wiping the sweat off my face, I turned to head toward the freezer to get my jaw some ice. A gut feeling told me to look over my shoulder, and when I saw him reach for my gun that I had tossed on the sofa, I instantly bolted out of the door. The sound of the man's furious shots echoed behind me, gunshots only making me run faster.

My heart was pounding as I took off down the street, desperate to put as much distance between myself and this madman as possible. I reached the end of the block and turned around to fall back onto the building, breathless and shaken but alive. As I leaned against the building, gasping for air, a car came screeching up to me.

"Get in!" Athena shouted to me.

"You bitch," I spat back with flared nostrils, "Your husband is trying to kill me."

"If you want to live then get in the car."

"I'm not going anywhere with you."

"He's a cop, Jim. One phone call and he will have this area locked down looking for you."

Shit. Inhaling sharply, I got into the vehicle and she sped off. Just my luck, the phone in my pocket rang.

"Couldn't have better timing," I answered.

That raspy laugh rattled in my ear. "Saw you had company and didn't want to interrupt. Have the lady take you to the airport. And don't do anything stupid, I'm right behind you."

Hanging up the phone, I told Athena, "Take me to the airport."

"You're mad at me."

"You could have given me a warning about your husband showing up."

Wearing a faded smile, "Last night I told him that I wanted a divorce. He didn't take it well. I don't know how he found out it was you."

"Well I'm sure your appointment book has me down enough times to look suspicious."

Cracking a smile, she nodded her head, "To be fair you always did get your massage. The happy ending was just extra."

"Why help me?"

The sparkle in her eyes told me what I already suspected. "It's my mess, not yours."

Despite no emotional attachment, Athena was a good woman and I didn't need to be harsh with her.

"You going to be okay?" I asked.

"I will."

Chapter Twenty-Two

The plane landed and I waited to be the last one off the plane. From the moment I stepped off the plane to the moment I got into the taxi, my body was stiff with tension. The sky was dark and it was thundering outside. I made sure I was aware of who was around me the entire time and whether there was a threat nearby. One part I didn't miss about being back in Chicago was the constant stress of being on your toes every second.

Seeing the exit to the airport, the weight of the stress was heavy on my chest. As I reached the door, it opened automatically and a gust of wind hit me in the face. It was downpouring rain outside. Running toward the taxi stand, I immediately jumped into one without checking who would be inside.

"Where to?" The taxi driver asked.

There was only one person here that I knew I could go to for me to peacefully lay my head.

"Take me uptown."

Soaking wet from the pouring rain, I knocked on the familiar red door. As it swung open, I looked up and saw Rachel in a robe holding a gun at her side.

She gasped when she realized it was me. "E, get in here."

Walking inside and straight to the living room, I closed all the shades before removing my wet hoodie. Someone was watching, I just didn't know whether it was my old boss or my new one. Rachel walked in with towels and placed them on the sofa.

"I thought you were dead," she said almost choking up.

"Guess God doesn't want me just yet," I replied trying to lighten the mood.

She took my wet hoodie, "Who says God will take you."

"The devil sure as hell doesn't."

"Afraid you'll take his place?" Rachel finally cracked a smile. "Jump in the shower, there's clothes in the dresser for you."

Rachel had been my go-to person for a lot of things. Advice, friendship, or the occasional fuck. We had our history but no matter what I had put her through, she was always been there when I needed her the most. After a long hot shower, I threw on a T-shirt and sweatpants then made my way to the kitchen where Rachel had a warm meal waiting for me.

"Your favorite," she smiled as she placed a plate of chicken marsala with bowtie pasta in front of me.

"Thanks, Rach."

She filled us both a glass of wine before sitting across the table. "What happened?"

"Got caught."

Rachel huffed, "Figured. He let you go?"

"I'm a dead man walking."

Rachel didn't need a play-by-play guide. She understood my involvement with Bethany wouldn't have ended well. I appreciated and respected Rachel, she always put me before herself even though I didn't need her to. She knew more about my past than anyone, aside from Cassie. There were things I told Rachel that I'd never tell Bethany – not because I didn't trust her… it was just… different. Bethany wouldn't understand the choices I made because she grew up differently. But Rachel, she understood me.

"Didn't I tell you if I ever disappeared to get out of this city?"

Rachel rolled her eyes, "I'm not leaving here. This is home."

"Rach, listen to me. Someone has been lurking around. It's not safe. If I make it out of this plan alive, I'm out of here and never looking back. You should do the same."

She straightened her back and carried a serious tone in her voice, "I'm not the one running from bad guys."

"That's because you were sleeping with the worst one."

Her eyes widened and she began gulping down her wine.

The front door opened and I nearly jumped out of my skin.

"Ma! I'm home."

The sound of his voice instantly calmed me.

"I'm in the kitchen," Rachel shouted back.

There was something about seeing Rachel's face light up when he walked into the room that made me wish I had a mother who loved me just as much as Rachel loved her son.

"Sonny," I said as I got to my feet to greet him.

"Uncle E," he smiled and gave me a hug. "Where ya been?"

Rachel cleared her throat. "Want some food?"

"Yes, I'm starving." He took a seat at the table while Rachel went to make him a plate.

"How's school going?" I asked.

Letting out a deep breath, Sonny rubbed his face. "I'm not even in med school yet and I'm already burnt out."

Med school. I'd never been so proud. "Well, no one said you have to be an overachiever and get into Emory."

Sonny smiled, "Go big or go home."

As we sat at the table, chatting and laughing as we usually did, the feeling of self-loathing began to eat at me as it normally happened in this setting. This was what I wanted – a family. I sacrificed being a husband and father for a life of crime. No matter how thrilling it was at times, in the back of my mind I wanted to come home to a wife making dinner as our children ran around the house causing a scene.

Sonny got up from the table, taking his plate to the sink, "I gotta run. Cecilia is waiting for me."

"You gonna marry that girl or what?" I asked.

"If she survives law school and I survive med school – maybe."

"Power couple."

Sonny smiled, "You always said to find someone who made you a better man."

"I wish you everything good in life."

"From your mouth to God's ears." Walking away from the table Sonny shouts over his shoulder, "See ya! Don't wait up for me mom!"

I waited until I heard the front door shut. There was a suffocating sense of silence that Rachel and I sat in for a moment.

"For such a bright kid, I don't know how he doesn't know."

Rachel laughed, "He's book smart, E. He doesn't have his father's street smart."

My promiscuous ways were always to ensure no one would catch on that Rachel and I have a son. It was too risky for anyone to know. In fact, it was Rachel's request to keep this a secret. It put a strain on our relationship although I understood her reason.

"Come with me," I hold Rachel's hands in mine.

"I'm not goin' to California. Chicago is home. I'm not leavin'."

"Rach, I can't leave you here pregnant with my child. Come with me. We can get married, have this baby. I can take care of us."

Her eyes water and a look of pain crosses her face. "I don't want this life, E. You aren't just working the streets. You signed on to be Luca DeCarlo's right hand man. The DeCarlo Family works hand in hand with the Baricelli Family. God forbid you cross someone and they come after our child."

"I won't let that happen. It can't happen. It's a rule."

Tears stream down her face, "What if you encounter someone like you? Who doesn't give a shit about rules?"

I sit down and let her words sink in. She is right. It is dangerous but I'm too stubborn to accept it.

"What are you gonna to do? Raise this child on your own? Let me make an honest woman outta you."

"I don't want to force you to marry me. I want you to want to marry me."

She thinks my feelings for her aren't genuine.

"You think I don't have feelings for you?" I question.

She places her hand on my shoulder. "It's better this way. You need to go to California and make a name for yourself. If I'm there pregnant, you'll be distracted. It won't do you any good."

Rachel had Sonny while I was in California and by the time I got back, Sonny was 7 years old. The top half of his face was all me minus the scar across the left brow. His manners were the same as mine. Although I was not listed on the birth certificate, ever since the first day I met him, I'd been around as Uncle E.

"You ever going to tell him?" I wondered out loud.

"Doesn't really matter at this point. You've been a father figure to him for so long now. But if you want him to know one day, that's okay by me."

"I think that would get complicated."

Shaking her head, "It's never complicated. Not with us."

There was a time I had deep feelings for Rachel but when she broke things off with me, I moved on. Throughout the years, she'd been more of a friend, one where the lines blurred at times. I took the moment to tell her where I'd been, what I'd been up to, and how I ended up back here in Chicago.

"We got married."

"You and the barbie?" Rachel's mouth dropped open. She always referred to Bethany as Barbie but she didn't mean anything bad by it. Rachel shook her head as she joked, "Always a sucker for big tits."

A laugh escaped my mouth in what felt like a lifetime. My tone remained serious, "I love her."

"I know," she replied.

"How did you know?"

"The way you look at her. The night on the boat – that fourth of July where you dragged me to watch fireworks. You were glancing in her direction the whole night every time no one was watching."

I took a deep breath. "You're a good catch Rach. I hate you wasted your years on me."

"Who said I've been waiting on you?" Rachel laughed as she got to her feet placing her dish in the sink. "It's a bit hard dating when everyone knows you still hang around. No one wants to think about what could happen if they spoke to someone so close to Emilio Pugliese."

"You deserve happiness Rach."

Rachel began washing dishes, "We both deserve to be happy."

Taking a deep breath, I grabbed a pen out of a drawer with a notepad. Writing down private information, I gave it to Rachel.

"If anything happens, this is for you and Sonny."

"E..."

"It was going to Sonny anyway," I cut in. "Just in case he needs it sooner."

Rachel looked at the notepad and nodded. I pulled her in and placed a kiss on her forehead.

"I am going to need a favor." I looked at her. "I need some guns."

Chapter Twenty-Three

The hustle and bustle of the city gave me a strange nostalgic moment. Did I miss this more than I admitted to myself? Watching a Ferrari pass by, my heart sank a bit. The little town of Mosfellsbær in Iceland was peaceful and humbling which was a nice change, but standing back in my city awakened something in my soul. It wasn't enough to come back though, so I shook off the feeling and kept walking.

This area used to be a no man's land before Luca got his hands on it. He turned it into Chicago's wealthiest area. At face value, you'd think it operated by the booming businesses but in reality, it was what happened underground that had the good money flow. It was like an underground bunk where shipments that contained questionable items were transported out of the public eye from one part of the city to the other. If this MC guy knew about this or even had access getting in, it would ruin Luca. Even with the D.A. on his payroll, if there was ever evidence that would stick and came to light the D.A. would be forced to press charges in his due diligence. The standing deal was to keep it out of sight and there would be no reason to investigate as long as the D.A. got a cut. Luca gave him pennies compared to what he was making but only I knew that.

Birdy gave vague instructions on the meeting location. I stood in a parking lot, dressed in an all-black hoodie and jeans. Keeping my head low so I'd go unnoticed, I realized it was the same parking lot as the bodega when I first met Bethany. Whoever this MC is, made me question everything in the city I thought I knew inside and out. It wouldn't surprise me if the mystery man chose this location for a particular reason. Everything he did seemed to have a purpose behind it.

A white 2005 Chevy Astro Cargo entered the parking lot and pulled up beside me. The door slid open and there was a man with curly blond hair and Birdy welcoming me in. The man had to be in his 20s, and was holding a blindfold and rope. There were only two seats – the driver and the passenger. The door that slid open was empty and looked like it survived a horror scene.

"You're fucking with me," I spat out. "I thought I was part of the team."

Birdy smiled, "That's up to MC."

Rolling my eyes, I stepped into the van and had Birdy tie the blindfold around my head to cover my eyes and tie my wrists together with the rope behind my back. Seated on the floor of the van, I leaned my back against the cargo as I thought to myself; either this MC was extremely paranoid or he was bat shit crazy.

Birdy and the blond jumped to the front of the cargo and we began moving.

"Goldilocks, you think he's as good as they say?" Birdy asked the blond as though I wasn't even there.

"Quit with the Goldilocks," the young man replied annoyed. "I heard he held a man by the balls over the Willis Tower because they crossed the DeCarlo family."

I smirked to myself as I leaned my head back against the van. There were a ton of wild stories about me and most of them were true.

Birdy scoffed, "There's not a chance in hell a man would survive that. Bless the hearts of the idiots who believe it."

I smirked to myself as I let out a breath of air. They were trying to get under my skin. Defending myself wasn't my thing. Whether you believe the stories or not, it didn't take long to learn not to mess with me. The more people feared me, the more the stories became believable.

"I hear he has 10 kids now," I chimed in.

"Exactly," Bird spit out not amused, "It's all bullshit."

The entire ride Birdie and the blond were chatting, trying to get inside my head but I took note of every stop and turn. If I was right, we should be at the dock. That couldn't be right. Why the dock? Luca had men all over the place here to secure his shipments. The vehicle stopped and both men get out first. I heard their doors shut and their footsteps fade away from the vehicle. When it was deadly silent, I attempted to pull down my blindfold using my shoulder and looked out the windshield. We were at the dock just as I predicted.

The sound of footsteps approached the van so I pulled my blind fold back up. The door slid open and I felt the gust of wind on my skin and the light from the sun shining through the blindfold. Then I collapsed.

As the fog of unconsciousness began to lift, I slowly blinked my eyes open, the world around me coming into focus like a hazy dream. The sharp ache at the back of my head throbbed with each heartbeat, placing my hand there and finding a bit of blood. Confused, I tried to sit up, my limbs feeling heavy and uncoordinated, as if I were wading through water. The dim light of the room made everything appear surreal, and the faint sound of distant voices echoed in my ears, merging with the pounding in my skull.

What a piece of shit. I got dragged into a van, blindfolded, and taken to a place only to get out of the van and end up here. Going to the docks was a ploy. They wanted me to believe I knew where I was and now, I had no idea.

"He's up," that raspy voice clamoring through my head.

Getting to my feet, my eyesight was slowly coming into focus and I saw Birdy with Goldilocks walking toward me.

"Was that necessary?" I commented.

"Don't mind Birdy here," a voice came from behind both men, "I thought it would be fitting to introduce myself but needed to hide my whereabouts."

Both Birdy and Goldilocks stepped aside so that the man could come into view. He was middle-aged, with salt and pepper colored hair neatly slicked back and determined brown eyes, casually holding a gun in his hand placed at his side.

"You must be the big shot MC," I said crossing my arms across my chest.

We were in some kind of warehouse but there were no windows making me think this could be underground.

"I've been watching you for quite a while Emilio."

"Typically my stalkers are women. This new territory for me."

He laughed as though we were friends. "I hate to have to force you into this but maybe this can be a positive exchange."

"Why don't you start with what you need from me before I consider anything positive about this. Don't waste my time."

"Your time is now mine." He approached me close enough to make his message clear yet far enough so that I couldn't lung at him.

"The only thing I agreed to so far is meeting you. The rest is still up for debate."

"If you don't change your attitude, I'll slit that bombshell wife of yours slender neck wide open and frame you for it." His reply was so casual yet I could tell he wasn't bluffing.

"Why am I here?"

"I need explosives. Enough to crumble a building into the ground. You have good connections with the cartel."

"Who's the target?"

"Doesn't matter."

"When do you need them?"

"2 days."

I let out a scoff, "That's not enough time."

"Make it happen. I need them delivered to 1400 S Lake Shore Dr."

"You want to blow up the museum?"

"Just the people in it," he replied nonchalantly.

"What about Bethany?"

The man shrugged his shoulder, "Get me the explosives and you get the girl."

"I want to know Bethany is alive and unharmed."

He waved to Birdy to come forward and when he did, he passed the man a phone which he gave to me. Putting it up to my ear, I heard light crying.

"Bethany."

Her gasp pulled her out of her crying and she shouted, "Emilio!"

"You okay?"

"I'm scared," her voice trembled.

"It will be over soon."

"Please—"

The line cut out from the other end. Handing the phone back to Birdy, I took a deep breath. As I heard the fear in her voice, a wave of anxiety washed over me, igniting a fierce protectiveness that made my heart race and my palms sweaty.

Looking to the man, "I'll have them by tomorrow."

A grin of satisfaction crossed his face, "Thatta boy."

Chapter Twenty-Four

I was given chloroform to pass out so that I would be taken back to the docks which was better than being hit over the head. Walking along the boardwalk, my mind raced with how I was going to pull off getting these explosives. Finding a bar that was a hole in the wall where no one would know me, I ordered a scotch and brainstormed. The biggest issue I had was my phone had all my contacts. It was in my suit jacket the day I had been caught. There was no other way to reach my exclusive contacts without my phone.

My frustration grew as I had no other choice but to ask a favor from someone I wasn't fond of; however, Bethany was out there, somewhere, held captive by an unknown enemy. The clock was ticking, and every second felt like a dagger in my gut. As I stepped out of the dimly lit bar, the heavy scent of whiskey and smoke clung to my clothes. The night was an inky black, the city's lights flickering as people continued to walk the boardwalk. I had always thrived in the shadows of the night; however, tonight I felt vulnerable, stripped of my bravado. Grabbing a taxi, I headed to my destination.

The taxi pulled up to a charming brownstone with a classic brick facade and arched windows giving a timeless elegance. The inviting entrance featured a stately wooden door, flanked by an intricate wrought iron railing that led up to a spacious front porch. Each step up the stoop ate away at my ego. I climbed the ranks through a mix of charm and ruthlessness; however, my approach must be humbling. I gave three knocks on the door and waited half hoping no one would answer; however, once I heard someone unlock the door from the other side I took a deep breath to prepare myself.

The door opened and there stood Hamilton Branton. Controlling myself from rolling my eyes, I stood there waiting for him to let me in. It was as though he saw a ghost but then quickly snapped out of it.

"How?"

Letting myself in, I pushed through and shut the door behind me. "Long story. But I don't have time to answer questions. I need your help."

The shocked expression turned into confusion, "To what do I owe the pleasure of your visit, Emilio?"

The thought of seeking help from Hamilton gnawed at me. Hamilton, the District Attorney's son—the very embodiment of the law, and the one person I never thought I'd have to turn to.

"Is everything okay?" A woman's voice carried to the foyer. A petite figure appeared. "Ham who is this?"

"Kathy, this is-" Hamilton shot me a glance.

"Jim," I replied extending my hand to her.

I was well aware of who Kathy is – born and raised elite who had been in constant competition with Bethany.

"Nice to meet you Jim. We were getting ready to head to bed. Is this urgent?"

Now it was me who shot a glance at Hamilton.

"Honey, head upstairs. I'll meet you there." He placed a kiss on her cheek.

"Don't be long," she replied with a tight smile then turned away.

"Why don't we go into the library," Hamilton suggested leading the way.

Inside the brownstone boasted high ceilings and original hardwood floors, seamlessly blending historic character with modern amenities. The large windows perfect for sunlight to illuminate the open living space, while the cozy fireplace provided a warm focal point in the heart of the living room.

Stepping into the library, Hamilton shut the door behind me. It was clear he was in here when I came, as the light was on and there was paperwork all over the desk with a glass of liquor almost empty.

"Why are you here?" Hamilton wasn't looking for small talk – and neither was I.

"I need you to do me a favor."

"Why me? Usually you discuss those things with my father." Hamilton's tone was teasing, but I could sense the underlying tension.

"Because your father won't do what I need. But you will."

"I'm not looking to get involved with whatever my father has with the DeCarlo family."

"That's why I need you."

"If I haven't made it clear – I don't care what you need." Hamilton stepped closer, his eyes narrowing. "Why should I help you? You're a mobster. You and I are not on the same side of the law."

Fighting the urge to roughen him up, I rubbed my hands together for a second.

"It's not for me. It's for Bethany."

The sound of her name made him stand up straighter than he already was and I knew I had his full attention.

"What's happened to her? Is she okay?"

"She will be if you help me."

Hamilton's lips tightened together as the tension in his facial muscles strained. "What do you need?"

"I need you to make sure charges are brought onto Luca."

The look on Hamilton's face changed as he realized the danger in the situation. "Have you lost your mind? Why would you want that?"

"It's the only way I can save her."

We exchanged a look only that fools in love do. Hamilton didn't need to ask why I was throwing Luca under the bus. We both shared a love for Bethany that we were required to hold back. We harbored this common bittersweet secret simmering beneath the surface filled with longing but suppressed for different reasons. That would be the only thing in common we had, and it bound us as we were both willing to betray everyone around to ensure she was safe.

"What do you have that will stick?"

"Shipment comes in tomorrow morning at 5am. Wait until the last cargo package gets unloaded. A school bus is going to pull up."

"A school bus? You men have no boundaries."

"You can say whatever you want but we have paid our dues around here."

"Infiltrating the streets with drugs and weapons – really making a difference."

Stepping closer to him, "You don't want to know the shit I've done to get your family out of so you can keep your pristine reputation."

I let it sink waiting for his tone to change.

"Luca has eyes and ears everywhere. As soon as there's a whisper of interference, his tracks are covered. My father will make sure of it."

"Figure it out. I'm going to do my part, so this part is up to you. Don't fail her."

"You understand that there's no going back from this."

"I understand."

Chapter Twenty-Five

The sun hung low in the sky, casting long shadows across the gritty docks where the salty breeze mingled with the scent of oil and rust. I leaned against the weathered wooden post, my hands stuffed deep into the pockets of my worn leather jacket, scanning the horizon for any sign of movement. I knew the shipment was due to arrive any minute, and with it, the tension in my gut twisted tighter.

The betrayal stung, but what choice did I have? This plan needed to work – too much was on the line. As the rumble of an approaching truck broke the silence, my pulse quickened and my eyes narrowed as I spotted the boat docking.

I stood at the edge of the pier, my heart pounding as I watched the boat slowly glide into the dock, the muffled sounds of the engine sputtering against the backdrop of distant seagulls. The morning sun glinted off the water, casting shimmering patterns that danced across the hull, but my gaze was fixed on the figures aboard. Feeling the weight of the moment, knowing that the fate of everyone involved hinged on the next few seconds— the boat finally nestled against the dock.

The crew began unloading boxes, the sound of crates clattering against concrete rising in the air. A siren wailed in the distance, piercing through the air. I couldn't take my eyes off it. The officers spilled onto the dock, shouting commands as they rushed toward the cargo. I watched large wooden boxes taken off the boat and onto a truck that was heading toward the police station. Pulling out the burner phone I called the only number saved in there.

"Done already?" Birdy's voice answered.

"Shipment is en route. You'll have everything you need and then some."

"Good. Goldilocks will intercept."

"Now, where's Bethany?"

"A deal is a deal but you have yet to return the favor."

My stomach twisted in knots. I was hoping they wouldn't use saving my life as a favor I'd have to pay back. If they didn't have Bethany, I'd tell them to fuck off. This wasn't proper, Bethany should be released and then I could return the favor, but these men didn't seem to have a code of honor.

"What now?" I replied with obvious irritation.

"I'm going to need you to get rid of Alfie."

"What did the kid do to you?"

"This isn't 21 questions. Just do it."

This MC was really becoming a nuisance.

"You need a handle on what a deal is and what a favor is. Deal was getting you explosives, I did that, now you return Bethany to me. You saved my life, I'll owe you the favor and toss the kid out of your way."

"You have a bad track record of returning favors. I'll hold onto the girl until you follow through."

Chapter Twenty-Six

Luca POV

"You have a crack on the inside," Cohen commented as we were left in a private room to discuss the issue. "I can argue these one of two ways. One, you're being framed; or second, if you know who has turned on you I can make sure they take the heat for this and not you."

Exhaling out in frustration, "Either way looks like I'll have to be locked up until I get in front of a judge."

My attorney nodded his head, "But you know the outcome will be in your favor."

"You understand Branton is practically on his death bed. At some point, he needs to throw in the towel and there's no one to take his place."

The D.A. was diagnosed with stage 4 cancer too late to catch. Dealing with chasing a ghost that had haunted my family and not having Emilio, there was no time or energy to ensure potential candidates were scoped out for the position.

"I'm sure his son Hamilton will likely be his successor."

I shook my head, "He couldn't give two shits about me. Made it clear he's looking to keep his political career with clean hands."

Cohen laughed, "He won't get far. Politicians who are well known and successful are just as corrupt. Only difference is the law makes you out to be a criminal."

"Wouldn't matter anyway. Should his father die, the standing D.A. to take his place in the interim of the next election won't care about me either. She's looking to make a name for herself, and having Luca DeCarlo on trial, she's going to have to pull whatever she can not to lose. You know how dirty they can be too."

A knock at the door took our attention, Cohen stood up to see who it was. "We aren't taking any pleas."

"I need to speak with him." Although the voice was muffled, I was able to make out who it was.

"Let him in," I shouted to Cohen.

Stepping aside, Hamilton walked in dressed as though he was ready to make a press release.

"Come to rub this in my face?" I shot at him.

"No," Hamilton gulped while walking into the room. "May I?" He asked as he motioned to the chair.

"You may," I replied wondering if he was being snarky or if that was how his manners generally were.

Cohen sat beside me as Hamilton took a seat across from us at the small rectangular table.

"As you may or may not know, my father is ill and his days are numbered. I've been handling all of his work as he requested so that you can continue with your activities in the city." Hamilton took out a pen and paper and rested his briefcase on the chair beside him. He looked at me with such distaste. Little did he know about the history of how the Branton family came to power.

"We don't have time to hear you rambling," Cohen stated.

Clearing his throat, "I want to speak to Luca alone."

Cohen looked to me for confirmation and when I nodded, he got to his feet and left the room. Hamilton was nervous, I could tell by how his breathing changed and his forehead seemed to glisten from the sweat forming there.

"I'm the one who called it in," Hamilton confessed.

When I leaned forward onto the table, he jumped back in his seat. "Don't worry," I mocked, "I won't hurt you."

"It was Emilio," Hamilton blurted out, not trusting I wouldn't rip the pen out his hand to stab him with it. "He came to me last night. Seizing the shipment was deliberate."

Hearing Emilio's name caused a vile uproar within me. I trusted him with every fiber of my being and it shouldn't have surprised me that he would be the one to betray me. But I knew Emilio well, if he was in the city then that meant Bethany was in trouble. My guess was ghost. He would be the only one who put Emilio in this situation. When Bethany left, her note was simple but when I saw Emilio's handkerchief that he frequently used to have with his suit left on the dresser – I knew he came back for her. She was safer with him until everything died down.

Emilio also never did anything in a simple fashion. He must be getting followed so contacting me would have been risky but using the D.A., or in this case his son, was a strategic move. That shipment contained a lot of illegal items and if I had to guess, ghost needed them for something, and to interfere with my cargo meant whatever ghost had planned was going to be coming up very soon.

"Why are you telling me this?"

"He needs you here," Hamilton replied.

A chill sent goosebumps throughout my body. Emilio was telling me I was ghost's next target, but if I was taken in by authorities, then ghost's plan would fall through. The pieces began to click. The monthly trio meeting was set for tomorrow. Ghost wasn't just targeting me, he wanted all three of us.

"Where is he now?"

"I don't know."

"I can't stay in here," I replied. "I'll take the risk."

"You aren't going anywhere. I intend to push as many charges on you as possible. Get comfortable in here."

Leaning back in my chair, I gave him a look that was quickly humbling him. "What do think this city would be without me? Hm? You think it'd be safer?"

"Less weapons, drugs, and other crimes."

I laughed, "I keep everyone in this city in check. If you think removing me will make this city better you're wrong. I don't flush weapons and drugs through the city for my own benefit. Every major authority figure in this city has their hands dirty. You'll have to take down everyone."

Hamilton seemed taken aback by this causing me to laugh again.

With a stern tone, I continue, "I keep these streets under control. Without me there would be chaos. You couldn't handle chaos."

"Try me."

"First person you will need to lock up is your father. If he's still around."

Hamilton tightened the grip on his pen, "Leave him out of this."

"Don't tell me you honestly think the Branton name was built honestly, do you?"

The hesitation told me he was clueless and was internally debating whether to open that can of worms. So I encouraged it.

"That scandal that never made the press. You know, the one where your father had a secret family?"

"What?" Hamilton reacted. "He doesn't have a secret family."

"Not anymore," I stated. "My condolences."

The look of mortification crossed his face. He knew. Trained to appear innocent but he knew damn well about his father's mistress and 3 children.

I wouldn't be surprised if he thought his father paid them to go away but nonetheless he knew they weren't going to be an issue anymore. But I wasn't going to stop there.

"It would be a shame if that case against your brother re-opened when the missing weapon reappears." I remained nonchalant. "Or how your father won the D.A. election."

"Enough," Hamilton stated. "I just want to take my father's place without having any ties to you."

"Well that's a challenge. I can't have you running around knowing at any point you'll be looking for something to pin on me."

"There's one way I guarantee that I wouldn't do that."

His reply caught my interest. "What would that be?"

"Bethany."

I hid the smirk from crossing my face. Of course my sister would be the demise of so many men.

"You understand she's a married woman."

"Well, you can take care of that."

"The apple does not fall far from the tree." I shook my head, "If you want no ties with me and have my sister then you will need to figure that out."

Essentially, I was giving him the clear to make Bethany a widow. Funny how things came full circle. You couldn't escape it. I needed him just as much as he needed me. That was the only way this city wouldn't go into shambles.

Hamilton POV

"I need a guarantee there is no one else that is catching her eye," I said.

Luca didn't seem to ask what I was referring to which meant he must have already known.

"*Luca was a fool to pass you up,*" Bethany says. She tries to convince me that for us to get out of our misery, we should get married, that my father and her brother will be happy, and that we will be free.

Unable to hold back my frustration, "*I did like you Beth. Really. But it doesn't take a fool to know when someone's heart belongs to another. I put the pieces together. I get why you tried to entertain me. Dangle me on your arm so Luca wouldn't suspect you were fucking Emilio.*"

Shocked, Bethany stays silent.

"*It was clear Emilio didn't like me. Hell, he even came to threaten me if I ever touched you again that he'd carve my eyes out. I figured that was supposed to be a message from Luca, but when your brother showed up to my father's house wanting to set up an arranged marriage – it threw me off.*"

"*Luca wanted us to marry?*"

I nod, "*His words were 'Keep the alliance strong.' It was set to happen and I tried to contact you but you just ... disappeared. I got worried and went to Luca. He said you were in Arizona for business.*"

I watch Bethany shift on her feet and uncomfortably gulp.

"*Luca never told me about the arrangement,*" Bethany confesses. "*I brought up the idea to him but he shut it down.*"

I rub the back of my neck.

"*Hamilton?*" She urges knowing I am holding back something.

My eyes meet hers as my hand drops back to my side. "*I called it off.*"

She lightly gasps in surprise. "*Because of Emilio's threat?*"

"*No,*" I reply. "*It was my call.*"

She gave me a questioning look. "*I'm going to need more details on that.*"

"*My father wanted me to go through with the marriage not because he cared whether I liked you or not. Locking in Bethany DeCarlo was securing his power on the city. I knew exactly who you were at that pool party. It was all planned out. Get close to you. Make you fall in love.*"

With a laugh of disappointment and a look of hurt in her eyes, "So you were just like everyone else. Using my name to benefit your own."

"That was my father's plan. I didn't care as long as that meant he was off my back. Then I got to know you. And I thought you deserved better than that. After a few days, I told my father to call it off but he refused. You don't go back on a deal with Luca DeCarlo."

"So then how did you do it?"

"I started asking around. Everyone confirmed backing out was a bad idea. That you didn't want Luca sending Emilio to offer the consequence of doing that. Emilio doesn't come to warn, he sets out for blood. That's when the pieces started clicking. Emilio said he'd carve my eyes out if I saw you again. That's a warning. For someone who doesn't give warnings, that had to mean something. So, I confronted him."

Her eyes widen. "You, confronted Emilio? About the situation?"

"That was the scariest 5 minutes of my life," I confess, still shaken up by the memory.

"What did you tell him?"

"I was able to convince him not to cut my tongue off right then and there."

"How?"

"I told him if he wanted me to keep quiet then he'd have to convince Luca to drop the marriage thing."

The look of confusion on her face is replaced by a distasteful glare. "We would have made a good team."

How could she look at me like that? I smile sarcastically and shake my head, "I'm not made for your kind."

"My kind?"

"My father may be a lot of things but we aren't criminals. Now that I know exactly what it means to be a DeCarlo, I can't be tainted by the image

I made for myself. One that I've tried so hard to separate myself from living in my father's shadow."

I turn around and begin walking away while anger brews within her.

"It wouldn't taint your name. Marrying a DeCarlo would elevate it," her words leave a buzz in the air. "After all, we are above you."

This made me stop and turn back around. "Above me?"

"Why do you think Luca keeps your father in office?"

"Your brother has him stuck in a corner."

Walking toward me, Bethany lashes out defending her family. "The only difference between our families is that mine is considered to be on the opposite side of the law. But make no mistake, their actions are just as bad. Morally. Your family's power is stemmed and fueled by greed."

"You're going to tell me with a straight face that Luca isn't just as greedy?" I shoots back.

"My brother is hellbent on making sure our family stays alive. It has nothing to do with greed."

"You're going to give me some mobster fairytale story?" I cross my arms against my chest, the fabric of my suit clings against my arms.

"It's no fairytale. Our family line did what they had to in order to survive. Life of crime wasn't the goal. The goal was to make money to put food on the table, a roof over their family's head, and respect to their name. Everything else was just what came with it. So, we may be the same in certain ways, but for us it always goes back to family - whatever cost it takes to make sure they are safe. Your father was willing to sacrifice you to keep him from falling off his own throne. Luca would throw himself onto his own sword if it meant saving us all. And because of that, we are above you."

Her words are a slap in the face. Can it be true that my family has dark skeletons in the closet? I know my father does but I always suspect it is because Luca forced him into situations.

"The untouchable DeCarlos. Yet they need the Brantons. Riddle me that."

"Because that's how this works between our families," Bethany looks me straight in the eyes. "We keep our hands dirty so that yours look clean. In exchange, you allow us to conduct our affairs without repercussion."

"You're lying."

"Your father owns a lot of factories in the city. He doesn't seem to have a problem filling products with illegal items as a means to transport as an exchange to keep winning elections." I start to sweat and get uncomfortable. "Should I keep going on how your family remains in their social status?"

"No." My tone is firm.

"Where do we go from here?" Bethany questions. "I don't want to be an enemy or a rival. I really do value our friendship - one that was made outside of alliances."

"You'll be dropping the DeCarlo name soon enough. Once you do that, I think we can get back to some kind of common ground."

"I can't control if she has a wondering eye," Luca said.

"You can make sure there isn't one lingering around."

Luca was right about one thing – the apple does not fall far from the tree.

Chapter Twenty-Seven

Alfie POV

"Take it like a good girl," I said seated on a love seat pulling on the blond hair so that my dick left her mouth and I could cum all over her face.

"Alfie! I told you no more cum shots on my face," Grace hissed attempting to find something to wipe the thick white liquid off her face.

"And I told you no more slutting yourself out to me."

Grace hated when I used a cocky tone but no matter how rude I was to her, she kept coming back for more. I think she got off on being with a younger man, and who am I to deny her fantasies. She was into just about everything – her favorite being trauma play.

With a devious smile, she replied, "Follow me handsome."

I followed her to an open area with a stage set up and a few people gathered around. A man walked onto the stage and asked the crowd, "Which lovely lady would like to be our muse for tonight?"

Grace wanted to come to this exclusive sex party that catered to her favorite sexual desire. I was willing to try anything once but made it clear once things got weird, I was gone. This game they would play tended to be over the top for my liking. The rules were simple. The crowd dictated your moves. They tell you what position, where to touch, and how much to inflict on the other person.

Grace stepped forward in her see through lace bra and underwear. The man smiled and invited her on the stage. Her nipples were poking through the sheer fabric as you heard the AC turn up.

A man addressed the crowd, "What kind of play should our beautiful muse here endure for the evening?"

I became uncomfortable as people in the crowd began shouting out answers.

"Orgy."

"Woman on woman."

"Rape."

The man on the stage nodded his head in approval. That was my cue to leave. As I made my way through the growing crowd, I found my clothes and threw them on. Grace found her way here, she could find her way back. It was cold and the wind hit my face like slashes of a whip. Quickly getting into my car, I felt an immediate shift in tension as I knew I wasn't the only one in the car by the sound of the gun click and the metal barrel against my head.

"Drive."

I glanced at my rearview and met a pair of brown eyes. "Do you know who I am?"

"Very well." The man's voice held a threat. "Now like I said, drive. And no funny business."

Starting the car, I left the parking spot and took his direction driving down the winding road.

"Who are you?"

"I believe you call me ghost."

My body tensed. Immediately I knew what he was referring to. He had been the ghost we had been looking for unsuccessfully. It sent chills down my spine knowing this person was in my backseat unapologetically.

"For a second I thought I may have had a stalker although I would have preferred a female – they have sites for that you know. Hurts less to know you'd get swiped left."

"Humorous," the man commented, "Tell me, does Aria still have those haunting dreams of me?"

"You've been long forgotten," I lied.

This was the man who left burn marks on Aria's back. We have been looking for him since without any luck.

"Alfie, is short for Alfred I assume. Is that a family name?"

Glancing between my rearview and the road, I replied, "You can ask the priest who found me."

"An orphan."

My hands gripped the steering wheel and the uneasy feeling was starting to bottom up a negative emotion. I had long stopped calling myself an orphan – the DeCarlo family took me in and cared for me in more ways than any foster family had. I didn't have it rough growing up like other kids, but I never got the close familial bond until I encountered the DeCarlos.

"Is that what you want to talk about?" I mocked. "Usually, people don't need to sneak into my car with a gun for that."

"I have a proposition for you."

"Bite me," I replied.

"Emilio wouldn't be so quick to turn something down without getting all the details."

"I'm not Emilio."

"Of course not, he's free from the shackles of the DeCarlo family. Shackles that you now wear."

I let out a sarcastic laugh, "Men would kill to have my place."

"Oh, I'm sure. If you don't believe people are already plotting it then you're a fool. I know you're loyal to Luca, but loyalty can blind you. Open your eyes."

"Exactly what should I be opening them to."

"You're the right heir to the DeCarlo family."

I let out a hefty laugh, "You're out of your mind."

"Maybe a little. But I'd never kill my own brother to take his place."

"How Luca got into his position isn't a concern to me."

"It should be if it's your father that he killed."

The words hung in the air, heavy and charged. I stepped on the brakes so that the car's tires screeched and the smell of rubber filled the car. Annoyed and feeling not exactly sure what, I turned my torso so that I was looking at ghost right in the face.

My jaw tightened as I sneered, "You have some balls making that statement. I was left at the Church, abandoned by my mother and father. The DeCarlo family would never do that to their own."

The man was older, middle aged, salt and pepper color hair with a beauty mark under his left lower lip.

"Family ties mean nothing to someone like Luca. You're just a means to an end, a way to keep his empire standing. He doesn't see you as family; you're just a tool."

The man was relentless.

"Prove it."

Lowering his gun, ghost nodded his head, "Figured you'd say that." There was a manila folder beside him that he lifted and handed to me. "Go ahead, it's all there."

Taking the folder from him, I placed it onto the center console, opening it to see what was inside. There was a news article with a picture of a man, woman, and child under a headline that stated, MOB RIVAL STRIKES

YOUNG FAMILY. Under the photo listed their names: Marco, Bettina, and Paolo DeCarlo. Looking at myself in the mirror, I couldn't deny the resemblance between Marco and myself. It could just be a coincidence, right? I pulled out a birth certificate that apparently belonged to Paolo. There were a bunch of papers in the folder, but the one that stuck out was a DNA test that showed results linking me directly to the DeCarlo family.

Seeing the disbelief etched on my face, the man answered what I couldn't muster to ask. "You can ask Luca yourself."

My heart raced, torn between the loyalty I felt toward Luca and the unsettling truth that was beginning to take root in my mind. There was no reason for Luca to take me under his wing or make me his stand in right hand man for the time being. Nicoletta DeCarlo, known to be cold to anyone who wasn't her child or grandchild, was always warm and kind to me. Recalling one time she made me soup when I fell ill. Bethany always took the role of the older sister. Even Emilio, at some point, easing his reigns on me.

"Why should I trust you?" I finally said with a trembling voice. "What do you stand to gain from this?"

"I want to end Luca's reign," ghost replied, his eyes piercing into mine. "I want to expose him for who he truly is. But I can't do it alone. I need someone on the inside, someone who understands his methods. Someone like you."

My mind raced. The pieces of the puzzle were shifting, forming a picture I had never wanted to see. "If what you're saying is true... if Luca really did kill Marco, my father..." my voice trailed off, confusion and anger swirling within me.

"You owe it to your father to avenge him." ghost's voice was low, but it resonated with a fierce conviction that struck a chord deep within me.

"I take it you already have a plan in mind."

"*Il codice* will be meeting in a month and it's Luca's turn to chose a location. I just need to know where. Simple as that."

I took one last look at the man, "Nothing is ever that simple."

He shot me a smile, "Keep driving. The more information you can give me the more effective this plan will be."

The dim light of the private room in the lounge flickered intermittently, casting shadows that danced across the walls. The smell of cigar smoke hung heavily in the air, mingling with the scent of aged whiskey that filled the glass tumblers on the table. Luca leaned back in his chair, looking calm, collected, and in control as he contemplated the enemy they didn't know was lurking in their city. I sat across from him with restless energy as I tapped my fingers against the polished wood surface.

"Luca," I began, breaking the silence that had thickened over the last few minutes. "A large shipment was seized by authorities this morning."

Luca's eyes narrowed, his brow furrowing slightly. "So when do they take me in?"

"Should happen later today. I called Cohen and made him aware, he will meet you at the station."

Cohen was one of Luca's attorneys - he was keen, sharp, and ready with a defense to get Luca out.

He poured himself another glass of whiskey, the amber liquid swirling in the glass as he contemplated the challenge ahead. "Have you picked a location for the meeting tomorrow?"

"Field museum."

"If I'm not out in time, Aria will go in my place."

"Aria?" Letting out an exasperated sigh and running a hand through my thick hair.

Since the Emilio incident, he hadn't trusted anyone except his wife Aria. Typically, a boss would designate at least two underbosses should anything happen, but Luca refused to do such a thing. The bond of trust with Aria was strong and sending her in wouldn't cause much of a stir. She was Lorenzo's sister and her ties with the Baricelli family made her a trustworthy candidate between the trio. The issue was that ghost wanted to get all three don families at once. This was the only way he would be able to succeed.

As we sat there, two detectives came in.

"Mr. DeCarlo," one of them said, "You're going to have to come with us."

Both of them were on our payroll and by their body language this was an uncomfortable task for them. Luca stood up, gracefully putting on his jacket and complying.

"There are a bunch of reporters outside," the other detective said, "We can go out the back if you want."

"It's fine," Luca replied as though this wasn't the ruin of him.

Getting to my feet, we all walked out together. The moment the door opened there were flashing lights blinding me from every angle and re-porters shouting out questions eagerly trying to be the first to get the scoop.

I nodded to Luca letting him know that I got it from here. My palms were sweaty as I answered my buzzing phone and I saw it was a text.

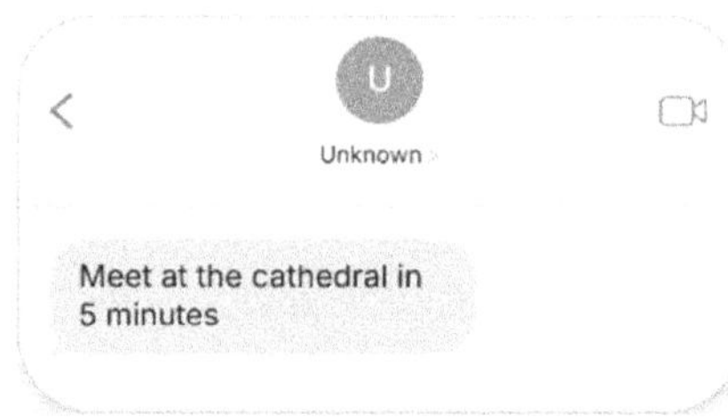

Flying down the city streets in my Ducati 1260, I parked behind the Church where I was able to enter through a side door just in time before it began to rain.

The dimly lit church, the faint scent of incense mingling with the chill of the evening air, and the faint sounds of rain pattering against the stained glass outside added to the atmosphere of secrecy. It was quiet without a person in sight. Walking around to the front of the alter, I looked up at the gigantic cross sculpture with a man nailed to it. The Bible said the man died for our sins saving us from damnation. I'd never been a religious fanatic – being a made man I found it hypocritical to be religious in this life of work.

Footsteps behind me made me turn around.

"We have a problem," I stated.

Walking toward me with ease, we stood face to face. "I know. Luca's been taken in."

"He wants Aria to take his place. I can have someone take the shipment out of authorities' possession that way Luca will be there tonight."

Ghost sucked his teeth debating whether to proceed with his original plan. "Might as well make it a family affair. Make sure Aria and Luca are there." Pulling out a phone to make a call, the muscles in his face went rigid. "Once he does the deed, kill the girl." I watched as he hung up.

Something in his tone made me worried. "Something go wrong?"

"Getting the party started early," he replied. "First DeCarlo down is Bethany"

We knew Bethany was with Emilio. Luca thought it would have been best she stayed with him until things settled down but now things took a turn. Emilio was working for ghost?

I could only hope tonight went as planned.

Chapter Twenty-Eight

Emilio POV

There was one place I knew I could find Alfie and that was the lounge. The air was crisp as the scent of fall was approaching. As I stepped into the dimly lit bar, the familiar scent of aged wood and spilled whiskey hung in the air. I held my breath as I entered the lounge that I used to spend most of my days. Although nothing changed, it looked different. Setting foot inside the place, I was half expecting to have guns pointed in my face but instead there was a deary feeling in the air. The place was empty.

"Took you long enough," Alfie's voice carried through the room before he came into full view. "Losing your touch, Emilio."

"You ungrateful piece of shit." Pulling my gun from my waistband, I pointed it in the direction of his chest.

My mind grappled with the weight of this betrayal that hung heavy in my heart. The revelation of this deceit would strike Luca like a thunderbolt, the kind that shattered the calm after the storm. Each breath felt like a leaden burden, the truth pressing down on me like a dark cloud. There was no going back from this after learning the painful truth. It would shatter Luca of any hope of humanity.

"Whoa, whoa," Alfie held his hands up – one held a gun, "We are on the same team here."

"That's how you greet friends?" I nodded in the direction of his gun.

Alfie tossed his gun onto a nearby table. "We are on the same team Emilio."

"I'm not on the team you think I am."

"You taught me to learn a man's pattern. See how he moves so you can try to dictate his next step." Alfie walked closer. "If we weren't on the same side, I'd be dead already along with Luca and the rest of the DeCarlos. You're the only one that would be able to pull it off."

"You're gonna look me in the face and tell me you aren't working for MC?"

"MC?," Alfie questioned, "You mean ghost."

I let out a deep breathe. "At least now we know who we are dealing with. How long have you been in contact with him?"

"For the last month, but it was to get close enough. It was the only way." Alfie stood tall and firm in his decision. "I got him to believe that I've turned on Luca. He trusts me. No one has gotten close to him any other way."

"Bethany has, she's seen him."

"No, she thinks she has. He hides in plain sight. You've probably stood right next to him without giving him a thought. He has someone else play him in front of people. Same features so it stays consistent."

"Shit. We really are dealing with a ghost. Are you sure you've seen the real ghost?" I lower my gun.

Alfie nodded his head. "I've seen him before. Like I said – hides in plain site."

"He wants the trio dead."

"Not necessarily. He wants the Baricelli line to cease to exist."

"What's that got to do with the trio?"

"*Il codice* was started by Vincenzo Baricelli who we know was a power hungry prick. But turns out he's sicker than we knew. He started the trio under the assumption that it will govern all families under 3 Dons. Each Don, however, is a descendant of Baricelli himself – something he didn't disclose."

"Jesus," I spit out. Talk about ultimate power. "So you're saying they were related to him somehow. That's one way to ensure loyalty."

Alfie shook his head to correct me, "I'm saying, direct descendant. As in each one appointed is his son."

My mind raced to connect the dots that would make this all make sense. "You know this for a fact?"

"Ghost said so himself." Alfie grabbed a bottle of scotch and two glasses pouring us each a drink. "Domenico obviously was his father's successor. But if Vincenzo was as power hungry as he was, then there is no way he'd give up his seat so soon."

"Not unless it guaranteed him ultimate power."

"Exactly, if the trio all followed his command, he would have all the power. Which means Luca is really a Baricelli."

"That's a far stretch there Alfie." I chugged the liquid in my cup.

"Think about it. Luca and Bethany don't look anything like their siblings. MC – ghost- whatever you want to call him, he said that Lorenzo's older brother Michael Cassarino was appointed to be part of the trio originally. He was killed. Marco, Luca's brother, was killed. But Marco couldn't have been Vincenzo's son."

"Why not?"

"Because the DeCarlo's didn't start working for Baricelli when he was born. It was only when Nicoletta fell pregnant and had a boy did the DeCarlo family become his Underboss."

"Where are you getting your information from?"

"Started as a hunch and then I did some digging. One thing I've learned is that women love to talk. And if you stick around long enough, they tell you more than you want to know. Nicoletta spent hours talking about her husband and how he came to bring them up from poverty. She talked about sacrifices that she didn't want to make for the sake of survival."

"What about the Cassarianos?"

"Aria loves talking about her brother Michael. Like it fills this void. She also likes talking about her Zia Stella who she spent years with in California. It's not a coincidence that your older brother gets killed and you get sent off across the country."

"So how did Marco and Michael end up dead?"

"I think someone found out and wanted to put a stop to it. Which leads us to ghost."

"But he still got to complete the trio with Domenico and Luca."

"And Morchetti. All current men are sons of Baricelli. And I think they know."

This was mind blowing, something I never even thought to put together. "That's why they didn't want Lorenzo part of it."

Alfie took it a step further, "That's why Lorenzo let Aria into Chicago. Why else would you send your sister into the lion's den? He banked on her either falling for Luca or Luca falling for her to secure his seat. If he's not their brother, at least his sister can seal the deal."

"Pour me another drink." I immediately gulped it down. "So this ghost knows enough which means he has to be older. Everyone has had an issue with the Vincenzo Baricelli, to narrow it down is impossible even with Domenico making many mends."

"Can I ask you something?"

"Not sure if I have any answers, you seemed to have really gotten your shit together while I've been gone."

Alfie smiled then it quickly dropped. "Am I really Marco's son?" Alfie said in a surprisingly calm manner.

"How did you find out?"

The look of hurt in his eyes caused me a shot of guilt. "Of course you knew," Alfie said under his breath.

Shaking my head, "I found out by accident. No one knows that I know. How did you come across it?"

"Ghost showed me proof I was. Said Luca killed my father and that everything I know about Luca is a lie."

"Don't let this baffoon change the reality of the situation. Luca did it to protect you. If the killer knew you survived that hit, they'd come after you."

Alfie nodded his head. "I know." There was a look of pride in his eyes when he said, "That's why I'm going to sacrifice myself."

"You don't need to do that."

"I'm a dead man anyway. Ghost sent you to kill me. He probably has someone in Luca's ear right now telling him that I'm the rat. I don't mind though. Luca holds a lot of baggage for everyone and he's done things for each of us." There was an odd look in his eyes. "He didn't tell me I was his nephew the same reason why he didn't call you out for being with Bethany sooner. It would potentially rip the family apart – and family is everything to him."

"He knew all along?"

Alfie shrugged, "Figured it out at some point." He chugged his drink. "You never leave clues behind unless you want to be caught."

I had to look away. There were times I did leave things behind hoping he would ask me so I could tell him – somehow I thought it would be easier that way.

"So what now?" Alfie asked.

"As long as we keep a tight plan between you, Luca, and myself then we may have a shot at getting this prick." I lit up a cigarette.

"How? He'll know you didn't kill me."

Letting out a puff of smoke, "You're forgetting a cardinal rule. Only believe half of what you see and nothing that you hear." Taking another drag then releasing the smoke. "I'm going to walk out of this bar. Once I have Bethany in my possession, she will contact Luca and tell him to meet here."

"Won't it be suspicious that you come back here?"

I get to my feet and nod with my head for Alfie to follow me. In the private room, under the table there is a secret door on the floor.

"This will lead to the river."

Chapter Twenty-Nine

With a gun in hand, I forced someone off their motorcycle. My heart raced as the engine roared down the street to the destination. It was an old building the city refused to have updated yet was deemed dangerous to enter. It didn't stop me from kicking in the door and running aimlessly to find her. Breathing in, my lungs filled with tension and fear mixed with stale air as adrenaline coursed through my veins.

"Bethany!" I shouted. "Bethany!"

I heard a scream coming from stairs leading down into a basement. Dashing down the steps, a few breaking along the way, I found Birdy and Bethany in the middle of the room. He held a knife at her throat while blocking his head with her own so I wouldn't be able to take a shot at him.

"I did want you wanted, now it's time to uphold your end."

"See, you made a deal with MC. Not with me."

"I should have taken you as a shady motherfucker."

Seeing Bethany tremble, the cold steel of the knife pressed against her skin, her breath hitching in her throat with every pulse of fear that coursed through her veins was gnawing at me but I needed to remain calm. Birdy's wild eyes glinted with a mix of desperation and madness, making it clear that he was unpredictable and volatile, amplifying her terror.

I had my gun pointed at him.

"You look scared," Birdy's rough voice had a hint of amusement.

"Not as scared as you," I taunted him.

"If I go down so does the broad." His grip on her tightened and she let out a yelp.

Bethany gave me a look. Managing to kick him in the balls, Bethany moved so I had a clear shot. Without hesitation, I pulled the trigger and watched it enter his heart with blood splattering all over Bethany. Walking closer, I shot again right between the eyes causing blood to splatter all over me. His body dropped to the floor. My face dropped with his blood and I wiped it with my sleeve but that only smeared it across my skin. Looking to Bethany she too had blood splattered on her. Adrenaline coursing through my body from what just transpired. Bethany's eyes glistened with unshed tears, her normally joyful demeanor dulled by the weight of grief. She was strong, but the sight of death had a way of stripping away a sense of innocence, leaving raw vulnerability in its wake.

"Bethany," I murmured, stepping closer, my voice barely above a whisper. "I'm so sorry you had to see this." It was nothing compared to her first wedding but knowing I had come just in time before he could slit her throat I knew was lingering in her mind.

She shook her head, her expression a mix of anger and sorrow. "I'm just glad you're here."

Bethany and I collided – our mouths locked together. Her slender arms wrapped around my neck and I swung my arm around her waist, pulling her further into me. My other arm hung by my side still holding onto the gun. We were getting lost in our own world, ignoring everything around us. Walking forward, I got Bethany up against the wall. The smell of blood in the air was making my skin tingle.

Bethany's hands made their way to my pants. Belt unbuckled. Button undone. Zipper down. My dick was about to rip through my boxers as it throbbed to be set free. When I felt the palm of her hand and her fingers wrap around it, I bit her lip causing her to moan in pleasure. My hands, with one still holding the gun, impatiently pulled her dress up, tearing off her delicate lace underwear. Her arms were back around my neck as she hoisted herself up wrapping her leg around my waist while the other wrapped around my thigh. My left hand was placed on the wall right by her head while my other dragged the gun up her thigh. I couldn't let it go, it was as though the pistol was a part of me. Adjusting my cock at her entrance, I looked into her eyes. Passion, lust, love all swirled in those emerald eyes making me feel weak.

Bethany was wet and ready to take me. We both let out a moan of satisfaction when I entered her. The inside of her pussy hugged my cock tightly as I thrust my hips against her. The gun made a sound against the concrete wall when I slammed my hand against it. Bethany clung to me as I fucked her against the wall. Our faces were touching as we just looked deep into each other's eyes. It took me by surprise when Bethany reached for my hand holding the gun, dragging it to her face, and placing the head of the gun to her jaw. The sight of this should have made me stop but instead, I went harder. Messing around with a gun while having sex wasn't something I thought I'd enjoy, but the sight of Bethany holding back from spiraling into an orgasm made me lose all common sense.

In a quick swift move, I ripped Bethany off the wall and practically threw her onto the ground then quickly hovered over her. Plunging myself back inside of her, she let out a loud moan that echoed within the small room. I held the gun against her cheek. It was almost like a blackout. All I remember was busting inside of her then collapsing onto her. My face buried into her neck as I tried to regain my senses, I wasn't sure if she even came.

Being demanding in the bedroom didn't mean being selfish. This was the first time I came without thinking about getting her there first. Sliding my body down until my head was between her legs, I positioned her right leg outward allowing myself more access. Wasting no time, I used my pointer and middle finger to part her lips. Exposing her sensitive clit to the cold air made her sharply gasp in shock. Her pussy glistened from being drenched with my cum and hers. My lips met hers and my tongue wrapped around her clit as I French kissed it. Bethany was already moaning and panting. As my kiss got deeper, my tongue rubbed around her clit and down below it in a slow circular motion. Moving my head lower, my tongue dived right inside of her. The taste of my cum didn't even phase me as Bethany was practically having a seizure. Glancing up, I saw her head was tilted back as she grabbed her hair. She did this every time I made her eyes roll to the back of her head. Using my tongue in and out of her, my lips on hers and my nose right above her opening, I continued to stimulate her until she was screaming out. Moving my tongue imitating a vibration sensation was driving her wild. The sound of my wet mouth on her wet pussy rang louder in my ears the more I went on.

"FUCK!" The word rolled off her tongue and out of her mouth in a roar when I replaced my tongue with three fingers inside of her. My mouth still worked on her while I finger fucked her brains out working my hand to the right position.

Grabbing her thighs, she knew I was giving her the green light to let her orgasm rip through her beautiful body. I could feel it coming as the inside of her tightened. Removing my mouth from her, I watch her come undone. Her cum shot out all over my face as her body jerked off the floor. The sound of her made it feel like the ground was shaking. I slowed down the pace of my fingers inside of her as she slowly came down from her orgasm.

As I got to my feet, I took in the scene around us. A dead body not far off with a pool of blood near Bethany – staining her blond hair. Blood had seeped onto her dress soaking up the fabric. Looking at lifeless Birdy, blood dripped from the edges of the body, pooling around our feet, a stark reminder of the fragility of life. But in that moment, the warmth of Bethany's hand in mine was a sanctuary against the horror.

"You okay?" I asked as I helped her to her feet.

She nodded, "Is everyone okay?"

"I'm meeting them in a few. Right now, I need to get you somewhere safe."

Suddenly a phone started to ring coming from Birdy. Knowing exactly who it was and why he was calling, I pulled the phone out of Birdy's back pocket. Sure enough it was none other than MC.

"You're too late," I answered.

"No hard feelings," he laughed. "You're free to go."

"You expect me to trust you?"

"You followed through and you are of no use to me anymore. If you skip town then this can be a settled score between us."

Chapter Thirty

Waiting by the river, I tossed my cigarette into the water and lit another one as I waited for Luca and Alfie. The night sky looked different from what I remembered. The contrast between the urban sprawl of Chicago and the untouched beauty of Iceland was profound.

Chicago transformed into a tapestry of lights against the deepening blue of the night sky. Skyscrapers punctuated the skyline, their windows aglow like a constellation of man-made stars. The streetlights spilled yellow pools onto the boardwalk, while the distant hum of traffic created a rhythm that pulsed through the air. In stark contrast, the night sky over Iceland offered a breathtakingly different experience. The landscape was draped in a cloak of darkness, unblemished by the glare of city lights. The air was crisp and invigorating, carrying the scent of earth and ocean. The Northern Lights danced with ethereal grace, ribbons of green, purple, and pink swirling in a celestial ballet, casting a soft glow over the rugged terrain. "Hey," Alfie grabbed my attention. "Luca should be here any minute."

"Where's Bethany?"

Alfie looked up. "My buddy Mark is taking them for a ride."

"Did I place him in the D.A. office?"

Alfie's friend Mark, who grew up with him in foster care, needed a job and the DeCarlo family was always looking for good help. Placing him at a desk job to oversee what happened in the D.A.'s office as an extra set of eyes worked very well for us.

"He got his pilot license," Alfie shrugged.

"Fellas," Luca's voice carried through the air.

This was the moment I had dreaded and longed for, the chance to confront the chasm my betrayal had carved between us. I could see the flicker of pain in his gaze, a mix of anger and disappointment that twisted my insides. We had years of working together as a team, aspirations and secrets woven into a tapestry of trust, and now, standing just a few feet apart, it felt like I was facing a stranger. The weight of my actions loomed large, each breath I took thick with regret, and I could almost hear the unspoken questions hanging in the air: How could I have done this? I opened my mouth to speak, to apologize, to explain, but the words were caught in my throat, knowing that no amount of explanation could erase the hurt I had caused. The silence stretched between us, heavy and charged, a fragile moment that held the potential for either reconciliation or irrevocable loss. No matter how this all went down, I wanted Luca to know I still would do anything for the DeCarlo family.

When we came face to face, he just pulled me into a hug. It took me by surprise but the act was so genuine, and I found myself returning the embrace. We were never this affectionate toward one another – we weren't made that way but it was a nice kumbaya moment.

"Okay, do you both need a room?" Alfie commented.

I shot Alfie a look as we pulled out of a hug. "Look, what got us into this mess was the lack of trust. If we are going to make this work, if, we need to be honest with one another. Can we do that?"

"Feels like couples therapy," Alfie commented.

Luca stood tall and glared at me, "How long have you been with Bethany?"

"That night when the Apollo brothers were in town," I answered honestly.

"Do you love her?"

"I do."

"You could have told me," Luca's brows furrowed.

"You know I couldn't have." I exhaled.

Alfie chimed in with his humorous self, "I'm pretty sure you said if you ever fell for a woman that you should be shot in the head. Would you want me or Luca to?"

His humor eased the tension making us l augh for a brief moment.

Luca, jumped right back in, "Why didn't you come back?"

"Because you and I both know you didn't really want to kill me."

"So I take it I'd be the one to pull the trigger," Alfie cut in.

As the conversation unfolded, a moment of silence enveloped between the three of us. Luca's gaze shifted toward his nephew.

"Alfie," Luca began.

"I know," Alfie replied. "I know. I understand. And I forgive you."

Their eyes locked, and in that instant, a world of understanding passed between them—no words were necessary. Luca's expression softened, a mix of pride and warmth radiating from his features. He saw the determination in Alfie's bright eyes, a reflection of his own spirit, and I felt an overwhelming sense of love between them. Alfie, sensing the weight of Luca's gaze, returned it with a hint of vulnerability, his youthful exuberance tempered by the depth of their shared history. The corners of Luca's mouth curled into a gentle smile, one filled with unconditional love and unwavering support, as if to silently remind Alfie that no matter the challenges ahead, he would always be there to protect him. In that fleeting moment, amidst the shadows of the night, the bond between uncle and nephew was deep—a silent promise forged in trust and love, stronger than any enemy they faced.

Now it was my turn, something that I wondered and never could figure out what the answer could be.

"That day you found me and Bethany. What made you both come to the house?"

Alfie shifted on his feet, "I knew about you and Bethany." He seemed ashamed of his confession. "I knew Luca was on his way to the house and I texted you to see where you were in case I needed to stall. Bethany said she made whatever cookies Aria was craving during her pregnancy."

Both Luca and I stared at Alfie with an impressive shock. While I was impressed that he caught onto me, Luca admired that Alfie didn't rat me out but rather protected the family – something Marco would have also done.

"How'd you figure it out?" I had to ask.

"The morning of her wedding to Pio, I went to check up on her and the room had sand on the floor leading from the terrace right outside the room. She was in the shower but I saw her nightgown was wet. I went to check out the terrace and saw Emilio walking up from the beach."

Now it was my turn to confess something I never thought I would but this was the time to. "I'm the one who texted your mother and sisters to come to the house." The dumbfounded look on their faces was almost priceless. "I figured if the women knew first then they would be able to make everything less ... intense."

Luca took a deep breath and exhaled. "Is that all? We got a maniac in our city that needs to learn no one runs out the DeCarlos."

"I'm clear," I replied.

Alfie nodded his head, "Unless you want to hear about the nasty thing Grace has me do to her, then I'm cleared."

Both Luca and I give him a push as we simultaneously bark out, "Never mix business with pleasure."

Clearing my throat, I think out loud. "We know that when there are too many people involved in a plan – someone is sure to spill. This ghost knows too much for someone who is easily under the radar in this city."

"There's another rat," Alfie replied, "Who could it be?"

"They don't know they are," Luca concluded.

He shot me a look and shook his head when he knew the person I was thinking of.

"It has to be," I replied.

Being Consigliere was hard, not because you were expected to carry out each order seamlessly, it was moments like this when the hardcore truth needed to be addressed. Feelings couldn't matter and I had to make sure the same applied for Luca.

"I'm missin' somethin'," Alfie commented waiting for the answer.

Luca let out a breath of frustration. "It's Aria."

Chapter Thirty-One

Shaking his head in disbelief, Alfie refused to believe that. "How? I've kept an eye on her. She always has someone with her." He gave Luca a look of guilt, "I've even taped her phone line."

"She could have a burner phone," I replied, "Isn't that how you kept in touch?"

"No," Alfie replied, "Not really. It was a meeting point. Nothing was ever addressed in any other form. That's why I can't believe it would be her."

"Who does she communicate with most often?" Luca asked.

"It's the same people," Alfie shrugged. "Close friends, family, her assistant."

"It's someone she confides in," I hit back. "Aria is the only person with direct access to Luca, Lorenzo and Domenico." The realization hit me like a bolt of lightning. "Shit," I spat out. "Grace. She's the rat."

Luca let out a brief sigh of relief. "How much could Grace possibly know?"

"Anytime time Aria needs to vent or needs advice – Grace is her go to. I should have known" I let out a huff, "She gives me intel on the Cassariano family. Someone good enough to be so close to a powerful family and not get caught giving information out is someone to keep an eye on."

"What happened to her owing you her life?" Luca questioned.

My debt is paid. Grace's last words to me rang in my ears.

"She saved my life that night when I came back for Bethany."

Alfie scrunched up his nose. "What are you talking about? Grace has never been to Bethany's house."

"She was there with Aria."

Alfie and Luca looked at one another before turning their attention back to me.

"Aria has been in hiding," Luca replied. "After you disappeared, I wasn't sure what you would do."

I don't blame Luca for thinking I'd go after Aria but part of me felt insulted that he had to think I'd go that low for payback. At the end of the day, it would be something I'd do, just not to him.

"Grace must have known about the secret pathway," Alfie spoke up. "Makes sense now. She made sure you got in and out quietly. Why was she there to begin with?"

"She was going to kill her," Luca stated.

"Why?" Alfie questioned. "Why go after Bethany?"

Luca deeply inhaled, "Because I'm willing to die for my family. I'd sacrifice myself every time, but I couldn't handle if one of my own gets hurt. Whoever this motherfucker is wants us all dead. Every single last one of us."

A group of people happen to walk past us.

"Let's take this conversation to a more secluded spot," I suggested nodding to the small boat tied to the pier.

Under the moonlit sky, the Chicago River shimmered with the reflections of towering skyscrapers as we quietly navigated the small boat through the dark waters. The gentle lapping of the waves against the hull was the only sound accompanying our hushed voices, each word wrapped in urgency as we approached a secluded spot beneath the North Avenue Bridge. Shadows danced across our faces, illuminated intermittently by the distant glow of city lights, creating an atmosphere thick with anticipation. We needed a solid plan to ensure we did this right – we had no room for error.

Luca, leaning over the edge of the boat, watching the reflections ripple in the water, "The monthly meeting is tomorrow. We need to separate everyone. Now that we know Grace is working with the enemy, we need to use that to our advantage." "Instead of tomorrow, let's get this show on the road asap," I said. "We know the enemy is heavily armed, but they're also overconfident. That's their weakness. If we use their own weapons against them, we can turn the tide in our favor."

Alfie, grinning, his eyes lighting up from excitement to finally be part of scheming, "Everyone needs to separate. If Luca sets the location at the museum as originally planned then ghost will think his plan is going according to plan. We separate each man sending half of them to the museum and the other half to a safe location." Luca, raising an eyebrow, "That's risky, but it could work. Only the enemy needs to die." "Ghost doesn't know the procedure for each meeting. So he can think the Consiglieres are scouting the area for safety measures. Unless Grace is made aware of that as well." "Not a shot," Alfie replied, "I remember my first meet with Giovanni, he's tough – like E here."

Of course he was. Gio was born and raised in Chicago – these streets were survival of the fittest.

"How are we going to separate everyone?" Luca asked.

Alfie answered, "Mark. Lorenzo lands in Chicago and we get him right on the plane with you and Domenico already on it."

"What if it gets leaked?" Luca answered knowing the possibility that having multiple people aware of a situation was risky. Alfie was on to something. Interrupting, I replied, "Aria."

"I don't want her involved," Luca replied.

"It has to be her. Aria speaks to her brother every day and she's very close to Dom's wife, Lina. It has to be Aria."

"When ghost doesn't see the trio at the museum, he will get suspicious."

"Only if Grace informs him. He needs a set of eyes on site," Alfie said. "Get Aria back to Chicago. Tell her to call Grace and relay the message to her brother since you suspect something fishy is goin' on. Meanwhile you call Lorenzo directly and fill him in. We get them here and then separate them. You get on the plane with Domenico and Lorenzo. E and I can corner Grace. I'm sure we can get information outta her."

Both Luca and I look at Alfie impressed.

"Told you he'd be good," Luca said to me.

"Not bad kid," I nodded to Alfie. "Alfie and I will find ghost's hiding spot and put a bullet through his head. Meanwhile get men to circle the museum looking for Goldilocks – you can't miss the kid, curly blond hair and sticks out like a sore thumb. Ghost is going to need someone there for a set of eyes."

"What if Grace suspects something?" Luca questioned.

"By the time she does, it will be too late," I replied.Alfie and I both looked to Luca as he contemplated the plan. "Fine. But I don't want a bullet through his head. Make him suffer. Gut him like a pig."

Chapter Thirty-Two

Alfie and I sat in a Mercedes 190 Evo II with blackout windows as we watched Lorenzo, Gio, and Grace approach the plane. Luca and Lorenzo exchanged words before they boarded the plane. A look of confusion on Grace's face as she realized the plans had changed. Looking to Gio, she told him something which in return he smiled then punched her in the face, causing her to pass out. Picking up her body, he walked her to our car and plopped her in the trunk.

As he walked up to my window, I slid it down.

"We want her back alive," Gio said.

"That's a joke," I spat back. "You think we'd let her live?"

"Trust me," Gio replied as he leaned against the door with his arm, "We have no reason to keep her alive. Lorenzo wants to be the one to do it."

I nodded my head, "I can't promise anything. We have a small, limited amount of time and I don't plan to start off gently."

"Just try to keep a pulse." Gio rubbed the back of his head. "Who's going to tell Aria?"

"Luca said to let her die a hero in Aria's eyes. Tell her Grace saved their lives by sacrificing hers."

"You ever heard, two can keep a secret if one of them is dead?"

"If you want her to know, that's on you," I put the ball in his court. "Start heading toward the museum. You know the plan."

Gio nodded and walked toward the car that was waiting for him. Three Escalades drove off, heading toward the museum to keep the plan going as though nothing had changed. Each one was meant to have a member of *il codice*. Ghost had to believe each one was there.

"This is going to work right?" Alfie asked as he began to drive toward one of our underground cellars used to torture our victims.

"You can't doubt yourself," I replied encouraging him to be more positive.

He couldn't know I was thinking the same thing he was. If this failed, we were fucked. Once we arrived, I popped open the trunk to see Grace still passed out. I hauled her over my shoulder and we headed down cement stairs to a door that led to an underground cantina. I plopped Grace on a wooden cross attached to the wall and tied her hands and legs to it. Alfie and I waited til she regained consciousness.

"Where am I?" Her voice groggy. When she realized her situation, she screamed out for help. "HEELP!!"

"No one can hear you," I replied calmly.

She hung on the cross like some holy figure. One thing I loved about this was that it spun around. I adjusted the cross so that she was upside down. This made her panic.

"Why are you doing this?" She asked playing innocent.

"Really Grace?" I questioned mockingly. "Playing both the DeCarlos and the Cassarianos like a game of poker. Did you ever think you'd get caught?"

A flicker of fear on her face as she realized her fate. "This is bigger than you and me." Her wrists bound by thick rope, she struggled to loosen them with no luck.

I stepped closer to her, my eyes narrowing as I leaned in toward her face, "You think you're so high and mighty with your little schemes. Now you'll pay the price."

"I wasn't looking to pick sides," Grace said with a shaky voice.

"Then why help him?" Alfie questioned.

"There are secrets that need to be kept buried." Grace began breathing heavier as she panicked. "Please, don't do anything stupid. Aria will never forgive you."

With a heavy hand, I slapped her across the face. The blood already rushing to her face from being upside down. "Don't use Aria as your scapegoat."

"It was all for Aria!" Grace shouted. "I was protecting her. Fuck the rest of you all!"

"What does Aria have to do with any of this?" I asked.

"If I helped him, he'd spare Aria's life."

There was this hidden undertone as though Grace was saving her friend's life not because of their friendship but rather because of something deeper. It was as though she was in love with her. Did Aria know Grace had more feelings toward her that went beyond friendship? Understanding wanting a love you couldn't have made me understand a part of why Grace did it.

"If you tell us where he is, I'll spare you."

I was disappointed that I didn't need to torture the information out of her but I could tell she wanted out of this scenario just as much as I wanted to get my hands on this ghost.

"I'm damned if I do and damned if I don't." Grace took a deep breath. "Alfie remember that warehouse we went to? You'll find him there."

"How do we know you're not lying?"

"I have no reason to. Once he finds out he's being set up, he's going to think it was me. I'm dead either way."

"Get her down," I told Alfie.

As we made our way out of the cantina, Gio was waiting for us. Propped on an old Mercedes-Benz W124 with the trunk door open, his demeanor changed when he saw Grace's face. Whatever he had planned for her was going to be bad.

"No!" Grace screeched. "You said you'd spare me!"

Alfie locked her in his arms and hauled her toward the car to shove her into the trunk.

"I said I'd spare your life. I said nothing about saving you from anyone else," I replied pulling out a cigarette. "How'd it go for you?"

Gio shrugged as he shut the trunk door muffling Grace's cries for help. "The explosion went off as planned. So this ghost should believe his plan worked." Nodding in the trunk's direction, "I'm surprised she was willing to easily talk. There's not a scratch on her."

"Grace knows she's dead either way. In her mind, she did the right thing."

We all get into our respective cars, Gio headed in one direction as Alfie and I headed toward the warehouse.

Chapter Thirty-Three

We arrived to a warehouse in the middle of nowhere about 45 minutes outside the city. The warmth of the late morning sunlight cast a golden hue on everything around us. The vibrant colors of the trees beginning to bloom in the woods, and the sounds of birds chirping fill the air, creating a lively symphony as I took a deep breath, inhaling the fresh air, and feeling the gentle breeze brush against my skin. There were various parked vehicles on the plot of land and although silent, the closer we got to the building the louder a thumping noise came from the inside. As we approached the entrance, the contrast became apparent. The doorway loomed ahead, a portal into an entirely different realm. No one was guarding the door which made it easy to just walk right in.

Both Alfie and I pulled out our guns and kept them in hand casually as we proceeded to move inside. Alfie pushed the door open and the bright daylight was abruptly swallowed by an enveloping darkness. Inside, the air felt cooler, almost still, as the light from outside receded behind us. My eyes struggled to adjust, and the dimness cloaked my surroundings in a mysterious shroud. Shadows danced along the walls, and the faint outlines of furniture and decor emerged like phantoms as we moved further in. It felt like stepping into a different time, where the day had been paused, and night had claimed dominion. The atmosphere was thick with a sense of calm, almost eerie, as if the world outside had been left far behind.

The low thrum of bass pulsed through the air like a heartbeat, vibrating the walls of the warehouse. Dim, colored lights flickered in sync with the pounding music, casting erratic shadows that danced across the concrete floors. The atmosphere was thick with the scent of sweat and illicit desire, a charged environment where inhibitions were shed like clothing.

We stepped through the entrance, our senses overwhelmed by the scene before us. Bodies writhed together in a tangle of limbs, laughter mingling with moans, the air heavy with the promise of debauchery. It felt like stepping into a dream—or a nightmare, depending on how one looked at it. I'd been to a fair share of sex parties, but this was on a level I'd never witnessed before. The kinks for this crowd involved more taboo sexual desires. But we weren't here to indulge in the chaos; we were here to find ghost. "Stay sharp," I muttered, scanning the crowd for our target. I could feel the tension in Alfie's posture beside me, the way his muscles coiled in anticipation. "How do we know if we have the right guy? I mean who's to know if I really saw the real ghost," Alfie replied, his eyes narrowing as we searched the writhing mass of flesh.

"Bethany said he has a birthmark on his left shoulder. That's our guys for sure." My voice was low and steady. As we continued to discreetly search the place, I could tell Alfie's mind was distracted. "How long did you know?"

Surprised by my question and unsure how to answer, Alfie shrugged, "About Grace? I had a feeling deep down."

"Why didn't you look into it?"

"How?" Alfie glanced at me quickly, "If I was able to prove it. How would I tell Luca his wife's best friend is a traitor."

"That's part of the job, kid. You gotta look out for the family even when shit gets ugly." My hand gripped my gun as I held it to my side causally walking and scanning the room.

"What I don't understand is why did ghost approach me? If he had Grace – that's the perfect cover up."

It was clear the burden of Grace's betrayal weighed heavy on him. I knew the feeling all too well; that feeling that it was all your fault. I never understood the allure of being a Consigliere, it wasn't a job made for everyone.

"He needed to know she was loyal to him. And he needed to know you were loyal to him. he used both of you as pawns."

"So, trust no one. Ever," Alfie let out a deep breath of frustration.

"The only thing you should trust, kid – is your gut." As we pushed deeper into the open space, the atmosphere thickened like fog, making it difficult to see more than a few feet ahead. My heart raced as I caught a glimpse of a tall figure with an unmistakable swagger, surrounded by a group of eager participants in the chaos. The way he moved, the way he commanded attention, was magnetic and repulsive all at once. When he turned around, I knew he was our guy by his birthmark. "There he is," Alfie whispered, pointing discreetly. "Let's move." With determination, we maneuvered through the crowd, bodies bumping against them, laughter and gasps echoing around them. My pulse quickened; every moment felt electric. It was moments like this that I enjoyed, and for a split second, I missed it. We reached a mass of bodies on top of one another. I surged forward, grabbing ghost by the arm, yanking him from the orgy like a puppet pulled from strings. The sudden motion didn't even have the crowd phased – they didn't flinch nor stop their activities. "What the hell?" Ghost spat, anger flashing in his dark eyes. Alfie and I held our guns to his body and when he realized it was us, a devious smirk crossed his face. "That bitch ratted me out." "Your time is up," I declared, my voice steady despite the chaos swirling around us.

Ghost's face contorted with rage, and he looked around at the gathering crowd, seeking allies among the few onlookers. But the revelers, sensing the shift in power, began to step back, the thrill of the fantasy was replaced by fear of the unknown.

I lifted my gun up and let out a few rounds. "PARTY IS OVER! GET THE FUCK OUT."

Naked bodies frantically ran around seeking an exit. Before you knew it, the warehouse was empty and all that remained were the flickering lights and pounding music. "You'll regret this!" MC shouted, his voice rising above the music.

"Who's going to come rescue you?" I taunted him.

Ghost knew his gig was up but he let out a bitter laugh. "You think you can just walk away? You have no idea who you're dealing with!" Ignoring his taunting, we proceeded with chaining him to the wall. Got to love when a party's accessories could be useful.

Ghost continued to lash out verbally. "Pussy can make you do crazy things. Like sleep with the boss's sister."

I punched him square in the face, but still he persisted.

"I don't blame you. She's good."

Unsure if he was playing mind games with me or if he was telling me he had a taste of Bethany, I knew I wouldn't let him speak that way about her. Another punch and blood began spilling out of his mouth. His victorious smile got under my skin knowing his intentions were to get in any final jabs.

"Good luck working for your father's killer," Ghost said now focusing on Alfie. "You could have claimed your throne but instead you stay serving as his peasant."

Alfie pulled out his knife and flicked it open. A sharp blade popped out shining in the dim room. "You lied. He never killed him."

"You're right. Luca didn't kill him. I did."

That struck an instant nerve and Alfie stepped up to ghost, and with a quick slash, under the belly from left to right, let his guts just fall out one by one. Ghost screamed in pain and passed out. Letting someone bleed out was never a quick death and that was the point.

"Let's wrap this place up," I said.

Taking the remaining explosives from the museum, we planted them all around the warehouse and a few close to the body. Ghost would suffer but we couldn't risk anyone finding his body. He would remain a ghost. Although Luca wanted him to suffer, I refused to leave without knowing he was dead for sure. I needed to witness it with my own eyes. We pushed through the door and stepped into the daylight, our eyes taking their time to adjust to the sunlight. As we reached the car, I glanced back, a surge of adrenaline rushing through me.

I took the keypad that controlled the explosives and handed it to Alfie. "Eye for an eye."

He took the keypad and nodded to me in gratitude. Ghost killed Alfie's father, and in return, it was only right that he avenged his father's death. The car was a good distance away yet we still felt a low rumble reverberate through the ground once he pushed the button. An intense flash of light exploded, the shockwave of the ground as flames leaped high into the sky. We remained still, breathless and wide-eyed, watching as the warehouse became a fiery spectacle, the culmination of secrets and sins consumed in a roaring blaze. The heat washed over us as we stood together leaning against the car.

"Did we really just put an end to this?" Alfie said, a mix of disbelief and exhilaration in his voice. I nodded, a grim smile breaking through.

"Yeah, we did. And it feels damn good."

Getting into Alfie's car, I knew either I'd be taken to the airport or taken to my doom. There was no saving me this time, and I felt that I cleared my name with Luca so what he saw fit, I would accept. Down the road, I saw Luca's car parked off the side of the road where Alfie pulled over.

"He wanted to talk to you," Alfie said to me. I wasn't even sure what the outcome would be.

"You've done a good job, kid. Your father would be proud." I patted the back of his head then got out of the vehicle.

I stood in front of Luca with Alfie behind me.

With a gun in hand, Luca raised it in my direction toward my head. "You knew this was coming right?"

I nodded my head looking up to the sky so that my last image engraved into my head would be heavenly clouds moving against the blue sky.

Chapter Thirty-Four

The gun went off and I felt something swiftly pass me. I blinked once, then twice, then a third time. Am I dead? Looking straight, I saw Luca standing there lowering the gun in his hands. He never missed.

"You could have run," Luca said coldly, "But you came here instead so that I can put a bullet in your head."

"You make it sound like it's a crazy thing," I replied with a light smirk.

Luca took a deep breath as he placed the gun back inside his chest holster. Neither one of us moved.

"You served me and this family even knowing that your life would end over it. You don't deserve to die in my eyes," Luca replied.

"You know loyalty is non-negotiable. If betrayal was forgivable, then the devil himself would still be sitting next to God."

"You forget the devil is a fallen angel. In rebellion, he tried to become God's equal. That's why he was cast out of heaven."

Surprised at his knowledge of that detail, I understood what he was saying. In no point in time did I ever rebel or try to take Luca's place when he'd given me power to be able to. He trusted me and knew where my loyalty lay without questioning it.

"So, I'm giving you an option. You continue your role in this family, or," I watched as he pulled out a set of keys from his pocket, "You start a new life."

"That's not how it goes Luca. Not ending me will make you look weak."

"To who? No one knows what happened aside from us, my mother, and my siblings. As far as anyone knows, you were away on business and faced a tragic ending. People know we always have something up our sleeves. It wouldn't be a shock if you resurfaced."

"If I chose to stay. What's the catch?"

"There's to be no ties with Bethany. Her and her husband will move out of Chicago permanently."

I knew I couldn't have it all but was it worth losing Bethany? Was the bullet still an option?

"Or you pick a new life with Bethany." Luca continued as he nodded behind him to his Bentley Continental. "The car has everything you need. New identity, money, and an account set up to live comfortably for both you and Bethany."

"She may not want to come."

"She's waiting down by the river for you."

There was pressure on my chest as though someone was sitting on it. Shouldn't I be relieved that I get to live and run off with the woman I love? Why am I feeling overwhelmed and unsure?

"You have my blessing. I know with you she's in good hands," Luca encouraged.

He didn't need to tell me that the offer was for a limited time, so I nodded my head.

"There's something you should know," I voiced as my potential last act of service, "If you just told me about Alfie, this would have never happened."

Luca nodded in agreement, "I know. I couldn't risk it, Emilio. He's the last of Marco we have. I vowed to protect his identity in Marco's honor."

"Even if it meant preventing this very moment?"

"Even if it meant preventing this moment. I owe at least that to Marco." Luca stood there waiting for my decision. "So, what's it going to be?"

Epilogue

"It's almost time," the wedding coordinator popped her head into the room.

"Thank you," I smiled with a nod.

Taking a deep breath, the last 25 years flashed before my eyes. It all seemed to go by so fast yet so slow at the same time.

"Ready dad?"

I looked up to see my son adjusting his bow tie. Getting to my feet, I walked up to him and gave him a manly handshake.

"The question is, are you ready?" I replied, perfecting the knot around his neck.

"I've never been more ready for anything more in my whole life."

I laughed, "Didn't you say that when you graduated law school?"

"That wasn't in the question you asked me," he laughed in return. "It was more of a ready to knock 'em dead."

Proud was an understatement about how I felt about my son. He was everything I couldn't be but so much more. He was book smart, but he also had my street smarts. He never dabbled in the lifestyle, and I was so grateful for his lack of interest. My children went to the best schools, dressed in the finest clothing, and I gave them everything they could ask for.

"Pops, can I ask you a question?"

"You know you could ask me anything."

"You think I'll make a good husband? You and mom set a high standard."

"If you don't, I'll beat the shit out of you. I just wish you took more time putting a ring on her finger."

"I know you think we're moving fast, but pops... she's the one. I've never met any woman who can make my heart beat so fast and so slow at the same time."

"I know the feeling all too well." I smiled and placed my hand on his shoulder, "I trust your instincts, son."

"You're gonna cry on me, old man?" He laughed but looked away, trying not to sniffle.

Gripping my hand on his shoulder sternly so he would look at me. "You're gonna make a damn good husband and an even better father. You made partner in the shortest amount of time at your firm, if that doesn't tell you something..."

A knock at the door interrupted us. Letting go of my son, we turned so that we both faced the door.

"We're coming!" I said. "I'll meet you out there." I gave my son a hug and walked out of the room.

Walking toward the ceremony area, Cassie joined me. "It's the big day," Cassie commented. "How are you feeling?"

"As long as he's happy Cass."

"Always thinking about everyone else," Cassie shook her head.

"E!" A voice from afar called out.

"Alfie," I smiled as we both embraced one another in a hug. "That California sun is doing you good."

He laughed, "Maybe if you get yourself out there, you'll see how good it really is."

"Where's Molly and the kids?"

"Molly had to stay back, so the kids stayed with her."

"Don't tell me she's pregnant again," I jokingly said.

Alfie laughed, "If she is, it's not mine. Got both my balls snipped."

"Sucker!" I laughed.

"I just saw Sonny and Cecilia. They are going to have their first grand-child. How about that ya old man?!"

"The family just keeps growing."

"I'm going to make my rounds and say hi, I'll catch you later."

Cassie nudged me, "I'm gonna go grab a seat. I'll see you in a bit."

I pulled out a cigarette as I stood by the welcome sign staring at it.

Welcome to the wedding of

Jimmy and Freya.

"Almost like déjà vu." Bethany stood beside me looking at the sign.

Her scent hit me and her voice was like a sweet melody. How she still had this effect on me after all this time baffled me.

Still staring at the sign, I replied, "Is it fucked up we never told them?"

Bethany let out a giggle. "I remember the first time Freya told me about this guy she met from Chicago. I just had this feeling he'd be the one. When I realized he was your son, I knew I couldn't tell her. I'm surprised you didn't say anything."

"How can I? It was the first time he came home and told me he found his future wife." I smiled at the memory.

"I wonder what Luca would have made of this."

"He would have been over the moon," Aria's voice said from behind us.

Bethany and I turned to face her. Aria never lost her touch, always looked her best. After Luca passed last year, she traveled often between Chicago and New York.

"It's good seeing you both together after all this time," Aria wore a warm smile.

I smiled unsure what to make of her comment. We watched as she pulled out two envelopes from her purse.

"I didn't want to do this today," Aria said. "But Stella, Marco, Lily, and I are heading to New York right after the reception." She handed us both our own envelope. "I finally got around to cleaning out Luca's desk. He had these two envelopes sealed. They have your names on them. I didn't open them."

There was a look on her face. "You know what they say," I replied.

She shrugged. "No, but I do know one thing, his biggest regret was not letting you both be together."

Bethany took a deep breath while I shifted on my feet.

"Mom!" Stella walked over in distress, "Antonio said I can spend the summer interning at DeCarlo Sites."

Aria let out a deep breath, "We spoke about this already." Turning back to us, "I'll catch you both later. It's going to be a beautiful wedding."

We watch her walk away in silence. Looking down at the envelope, I could tell this was written years ago. The paper was off white and felt old.

"I miss him," Bethany said, "Despite it all. He was a good brother."

"It wasn't his fault," I replied.

"I know." She turned to face me. "Do you regret it?"

I was hoping she'd never have the opportunity to ask me this because she wasn't going to like the answer.

"No," I replied still facing forward.

"I see," Bethany's voice was low.

Turning to face her, I looked her straight in the eyes. "I'll never regret making the choice to keep you safe. As Consigliere I have immunity, if I gave up the title you have no idea what enemies we would have to run from. That's not a life you deserve to live."

Bethany's eyes began to water, "That wasn't your choice to make."

A knot formed in my throat, "It was the best choice for me."

"Ah, there you are!" Hamilton joined us pulling Bethany in for a kiss then turned to me for a handshake. "Emilio, looking sharp as always. Where's the Mrs.?"

"Rach is probably running around making sure everything is going smoothly," I replied.

"Beth, you mind checking on Freya? Wedding coordinator thinks she's getting cold feet."

Bethany laughed, "Let me go see her before her friends get her drunk."

Before walking away, we gave each other a final look. However things panned out, we were all able to live a good and happy life even if it wasn't what we originally hoped for. I didn't regret allowing Bethany to get out of Luca's reigns and marry Hamilton after Pio was found dead. I was happy she got to have a family and live happily and peacefully away from me and this city.

Bethany walked away, but Hamilton remained. There was never a competitive moment between us since that day I asked for his help.

"Thank you," Hamilton extended his hand to me.

"For?"

"For respecting me enough to not interfere with our marriage."

"You made her happy so I can't complain."

"You and I know if you wanted, you'd still be able to take her away from me."

"Lucky for you, I'm not that kind of man."

Hamilton smiled and nodded his head. "I'll see you at the ceremony."

Left alone in my own thoughts, I played with the envelope debating whether to open it. Tossing my cigarette on the ground, I found myself taking the letter out.

The first line already choked me up.

E,

If you're Reading this, that means you outlived me you bastard.

I laughed out loud - partially because I always thought he had too nice of handwriting for a man.

E,

If you're Reading this, that means you outlived me you bastard.

There's always been a part of me that will hold it against you for not choosing my sister. I was hoping you'd be selfish enough to run off with her when I gave you my blessing. Instead, you stayed.

Marco was right, I could always count on you. You never failed me and I am forever grateful.

Maybe one day you will \be selfish enough to be happy.

See you on the other side, friend.
Luca

One of the hotel attendants approached me, "Mr. Pugliese, I'm sorry to bother you, but you're needed in the groom's suite."

I furrowed my brow. "Is something wrong?"

"I believe it's for photos. "

Rolling my eyes, I headed toward the suite. How many photos do they need? Strolling passed the incoming guests, I headed back into the hotel and toward the suite. Opening the door, I find Bethany there in nothing but heels.

Author's Note

Dear Readers,

As I reach the conclusion of this series, I find myself reflecting on the journey of Emilio and Bethany. These two characters are the epitome of two lovers forbidden to indulge in their desires. I wanted that to hold true throughout their storyline. Condemned is where boundaries blur and inhibitions fade yet reality snaps them back into place.

One of my greatest joys in storytelling is creating narratives that leave you with lingering thoughts—questions that echo in your mind long after the last chapter is finished. I wasn't just looking to entertain your imagination but also invite you to explore deeper themes, emotions, and possibilities. I hope you find yourself reflecting on the choices the characters made, pondering what their futures might hold, and imagining your own interpretations of their journeys.

In contemplating the ending, I want to share a little insight into my thought process. While I had my own vision for how the series would conclude, I ultimately decided to leave the ending open to interpretation. I believe that each of you carries your own unique desires and dreams for what a "happily ever after" looks like, and I wanted to honor that by allowing you the freedom to shape the conclusion in your minds. I enjoy creating these moments where the conclusion is not strictly defined, encouraging you to weave your own narratives into the fabric of the story.

Thank you for joining me on this journey and for your unwavering support.

With all my best,
Marianna
P.S. For those interested in the original epilogue, turn the page!

Original Epilogue

Drip. Drip. Drip.

The loud sound of water dripping into a puddle woke me. The shackles around my wrists and feet clanked together as I tried to remove them unsuccessfully. Taking a deep breath, I shut my eyes and say a prayer. Let me survive another day.

Drip. Drip. Drip.

A door opening and shutting woke me up. Desperate for some kind of human interaction, I wait to see who appears before me. It was dim in here. Footsteps get closer but no one appears.

Drip. Drip. Drip.

With no window, who knows if it's day or night. I don't even know how long I've been in here.

Drip. Drip. Drip.

There was no glimpse of hope at the sound of footsteps. Convinced I was just hallucinating I remained seated. When two men enter the room with flashlights, I barely flinch.

"Is he alive?"

"Go check."

I can see the person approaching but it wasn't until they placed their hand on my neck to check my breathing did it dawn on me that this was real.

"He's alive."

I realize it's Alfie kneeled in front of me and when we make eye contact, I knew this would finally be over. Plenty of times have I been on the other side of the situation and I wondered if the lives of the people I've taken looked to me with hope or defeat.

Alfie remains on his knee as the man stands beside him. Off the bat I didn't recognize the man although he looked familiar. Was it Luca or was it MC? It was too dim to make out any distinct features, yet then again, my fogged brain couldn't function properly from the dehydration.

"I won't be able to carry his body out of here," Alfie says looking up to him.

"Then just let him rot here," the man replies.